SPIRIT OF STEAMBOAT

CRAIG JOHNSON

SPIRIT OF STEAMBOAT

VIKING

VIKING
Published by the Penguin Group
Penguin Group (USA) Inc., 375 Hudson Street,
New York, New York 10014, USA

USA | Canada | UK | Ireland | Australia | New Zealand | India | South Africa | China

Penguin Books Ltd, Registered Offices: 80 Strand, London WC2R 0RL, England
For more information about the Penguin Group visit penguin.com

LIBRARY OF CONGRESS CATALOGING-IN-PUBLICATION DATA

Johnson, Craig, 1961-
    Spirit of steamboat : a Walt Longmire story / Craig Johnson.
      pages cm.
    ISBN 978-0-670-01578-8
    1. Longmire, Walt (Fictitious character)—Fiction. 2. Sheriffs--Fiction. I. Title.
    PS3610.O325S65 2013
    813'.6—dc23   2013017053

Printed in the United States of America
1   3   5   7   9   10   8   6   4   2

Book design by Alissa Amell

For Glenn Johnson, who always made sure
we straightened up and flew right.

You don't concentrate on risks. You concentrate on results. No risk is too great to prevent the necessary job from getting done.

—Chuck Yeager

Never wait for trouble.

—Chuck Yeager

ACKNOWLEDGMENTS

Spirit of Steamboat is an odd little book, in that it was supposed to be a short story, but within four days had spread its wingspan to over eighty pages. After a brief conference with Kathryn Court over at Viking Penguin, we decided to bring it out as a hardback novella, not exactly a novel. *Spirit of Steamboat* is about half the length of one of my Walt Longmire mystery books. As usual with my shorter pieces, it's not a mystery per se, but rather an adventure/thriller with mysterious elements; sometimes it's not so much about the suspense of killing characters off in a book, but rather, of trying to keep them alive.

I've always been interested in the World War II period aircraft, piston-driven, supercharged, nose art and all, and especially the Doolittle Raiders, to whom I pay homage in the character of Lucian Connally. I remember going to one of their reunions in San Antonio with Mary Brannaman's father before his passing; Bill Bower was one of those valiant men. There was a flight of magnificently restored Mitchell B-25's gleaming in the sun on the tarmac, and a group of pilots excited to take us all on a demonstration flight. As we trooped past the flight line, I happened to notice Colonel Bill watching us approach the roaring, high-speed medium bombers. "Bill, aren't you coming?"

He smiled as he surveyed the beautifully restored aircraft and shouted back to me, "I've flown those damn things and I know how dangerous they can be—you kids have a nice time."

Besides the usual crew members, I picked up a few hangar sweepers on this trip. There were a number of areas of expertise where I needed a little in-air assistance, and I'm glad to say that these folks helped me bring *Spirit of Steamboat* in for a safe landing in your hands.

First up is pilot extraordinaire and flight legend Duane Powers of Hawkins & Powers in Greybull, Wyoming, who kept my feet on the pedals during this flight of fancy. Those meetings at Lisa's Restaurant were indispensable, my friend. Thanks to buddy Mike Pilch and to Tom Malyurek for the debriefings at Perkins—jeez, you'd think that all I did was hang out with pilots in restaurants . . .

Thanks to Master Sergeant Eric Grim of the South Dakota Air and Space Museum in Rapid City, South Dakota, current home of the 28th Bomb Wing and the 37th Bomb Group, the descendants of both Lucian's and Bill Bower's 37th Bombardment Squadron—and the current home of B-25 34030, a.k.a. *Steamboat*. Go by and see her and pat her hooves.

Next in line, Dr. David Nickerson, the guy I turn to for all things medical; his pages of descriptions with handy diagrams made getting *western* with the assorted fiascos that attempted to thwart the flight of *Steamboat* remain both realistic and terrifying. Thanks to Dr. Frank Carlton for the guiding hand and steady reassurance in moments of stress—the Taylor's bourbon might've helped.

A thumbs-up to Candy Moulton and her fantastic book *Steamboat: Legendary Bucking Horse* for providing a true and articulate account of Wyoming's indomitable mascot. Thanks to Mary Brannaman for providing me access to her father's intimate knowledge and his genuine, horsehide, A2 flight jacket with 37th Bombardment Squadron patch attached.

Steamboat was one tough hombre to handle, but I had my usual crew to help me get over the turbulence—navigator Gail "Gunny" Hochman and radio operator Marianne "Sparks" Merola, pilot Kathryn "Cockney Sparrow" Court and copilot Tara "Spanky" Singh, nose gunner Barbara "Cyclone" Campo, and tail gunner Scott "Cowboy" Cohen. When the enemy was spotted on the horizon, I knew I could count on waist gunners Carolyn "Cat's Eyes" Colburn and Angie "Mad Major" Messina, top-turret gunner Maureen "Dizzy" Donnelly, and bombardier Ben "Pappy" Petrone, who always comes in on target.

And finally to my wife, Judy "The Jewel" Johnson, the fuel in my tanks, the wind under my wings, and the homing signal and landing lights that always bring me in safe.

1

It was Tuesday, the day before Christmas, and I wasn't expecting visitors. I stared at my archnemesis, the little red light on my phone that connected me via the intercom to my dispatcher, Ruby, in the other room. If I raised my voice through the open door—even over the drone of the lite-jazz Christmas carols playing in the background—the reception would be better, but Ruby is a stickler for procedure, so I push the button except for emergencies.

I stared out the window at the fat, heavy flakes falling like in a snow globe; it had been windy in the morning, but there hadn't been too many accidents on the county's snow-covered roadways, and with the updated weather reports, it was looking more and more like it was going to be a peaceful and quiet Christmas—something I rarely got in my business. I had no plans—my undersheriff, Victoria Moretti, and her mother, Lena, had decided to go to Belize for Christmas, and my daughter, Cady, was expecting my first grandchild in January and was too pregnant to travel. I was looking forward to the postholidays when Henry and I would fly to Philadelphia to meet the baby, whose name was to be Lola. I had thought her name was to be Martha after my late wife, but Cady had decided on Lola and that was, as they say, that.

I placed my book flat on my desk, words up, the weight of the sentiment holding it open. Taking a sip from my chipped Denver Broncos coffee mug, I punched the button. "Do I know her?"

There was a pause, and then Ruby came back on. "She says probably not." I waited, and I guess she felt prompted to add, "The young woman is carrying something."

"Smaller than a bread box but bigger than a subpoena?"

"Walter."

I glanced up at the old Seth Thomas on the wall and figured I had another twenty minutes of daylight on the taxpayer's dollar. "I'm doing my annual holiday reading; where is Saizarbitoria?"

"Checking on a drive-off at the Kum & Go." Or, as Vic liked to call it, the Ejaculate & Evacuate. "I've also got Lucian on line two; he wants to know if you are still playing chess tonight."

I thought about the old Doolittle Raider as I reached down and petted Dog, who was sleeping, lying low in hopes of avoiding the reindeer antlers Ruby sometimes attached to his head. "Why, has he succumbed to his usual blue Christmas?"

"Possibly."

I thought about how chess night had evolved from Lucian's poker games of yore, how the old Raider's companions had died off one by one, and how he'd been left with only two regular visitors and Dog and I didn't play poker. "Isn't that what old widowers do? Sure, tell him I'll be there."

It wasn't what I really wanted to do with my Christmas Eve, but with both Cady and Vic away, I was without female companionship for the holidays. Normally I would've headed out to the Red Pony Bar & Grill to spend the evening with my good friend Henry Standing Bear, but he'd been spending time up on the Rocky Boy Reservation with a young divorcée these past couple of weeks—the dog who wouldn't stay on the porch.

The season was taking a toll on all of us as it usually did, but I told Ruby to send the woman in. I glanced down at my book and read the line ". . . no space of regret can make amends for one life's opportunity misused. . . ." I patted my ancient copy of *A Christmas Carol* and stood to accept the visitor.

A dark-haired woman dressed in jeans and a long, elegant black wool coat stood in the doorway—she was clutching a garment bag and smiling a nervous smile, and was small and delicately boned with pale skin and what looked like a hairline crack in the porcelain of her forehead, almost as if she'd been made of china and at one point dropped.

"Please, come in." She nodded, stepping through the doorway, and studied Dog, who rose, stretched, and yawned. "Won't you have a seat?" Her hand rested on Dog's head as he sniffed her. I didn't have a lot of time and figured that since it was Christmas Eve, she didn't either. "How can I help you?"

"Are you the sheriff of Absaroka County?"

"I am." I spun my hat, which, when not on my head, was in its usual spot on the edge of my desk. "And you are?"

She glanced around my office, her eyes lighting on the Dickens. "You haven't finished that book yet?"

An odd question, but evidently she didn't want to give out with her name. I glanced down at the small, hand-bound copy with the gilt lettering, a Christmas gift from my father to me when I was fifteen and he thought I needed to understand the goodness of charity and humility. "Holiday reading; a tradition of mine."

"I know." I thought I could discern a slight whistling noise within her voice as she spoke.

I stepped around my desk and extended a hand. "I'm sorry, but have we met?"

The smile returned, but her hands still clutched the garment bag's black vinyl like talons on a branch; I noticed it had the name of a San Francisco dry cleaning service with an address at Taylor and Clay printed on the front. "You don't remember me."

The whistling was there again, as if some wind from another time and place punctuated her speech. Studying her face, I could see something familiar there, something from a while back maybe, but nothing I could really identify. "I'm sorry, but not really."

She looked at her feet, a small puddle of melted slush from her shoes surrounding them, and then back to me. "How long have you been the sheriff?"

It was an odd question from someone who purported to know me. "Almost a quarter century—"

"Who was the sheriff before you?"

Still feeling as if I should recognize her, I answered, "A man by the name of Lucian Connally." I watched her face, but there was no recognition there. "Do you mind telling me what this is all about, ma'am?"

"Is he around?"

I smiled. "Um, no."

"Do you have a photograph of him that I could see, please?"

I stood there, looking down at her, and stuffed my hands in the pockets of my jeans. There weren't any warning bells going off in my head, but the fact that she hadn't given me her name or a specific reason why she was here was keeping me off balance. I didn't move at first but then stepped past her toward the doorway; Dog padded after me, his claws making clacking sounds on the wide-wood-planked floor of the old Carnegie library that served as our office. I motioned for her to accompany us.

Ruby watched as we walked past the painting of Andrew Carnegie himself to the marble landing. I took three steps down and turned so that I could look straight at the young woman, who had maintained a two-foot distance behind me, gesturing toward the wall where the 8×10s of all the sheriffs of the county since its inception in 1894 hung diagonally in a rogue's gallery.

Mine was last, with a chocolate-brown hat and the ridiculous mustache and sideburns I'd had in the eighties when I'd first been elected. The photo was a color monstrosity that looked garish and déclassé next to Lucian's classic black and white.

His had been taken in the late forties a few years after the war—the good one, if there was such a thing. It was right before he lost his leg to Basque bootleggers, and he wore his traditional light-colored Open Road Stetson, a dark tie, and an old Eisenhower jacket, star attached. He was looking straight at the camera with an elbow resting on a raised knee, the other hand drawing the wool back to reveal the .38 service revolver he'd carried all those years, the one with the lanyard loop on the butt.

He wore a slight smirk with an eyebrow cocked like a Winchester, which gave the impression that, if unsatisfied with the resulting photograph, he was fully prepared to shoot the photographer.

I gestured toward the portrait in the cheap filigree discount-store frame. "My predecessor, the High Sheriff, Lucian A. Connally."

"High Sheriff?"

I glanced up at Ruby, who was watching us intently. "An old term they used to use."

One of the woman's hands disengaged from the garment bag and rose to the glass surface to rest a few fingertips there. Her head dropped a bit, but her eyes stayed on the image of the old warhorse.

I felt something pull at me again as I studied her profile, sure that I had seen her before. Drawing on my experience in Vietnam to help me discern Asian features, I could tell she was not Vietnamese or Chinese—Japanese maybe. "Miss?"

She shuddered for an instant, as if I'd shocked her by reminding her of my presence, and then turned with tears in her dark eyes. "He's dead?"

I laughed. "Oh God, no . . ." I glanced up at Ruby, who continued to study the woman with more than some interest. "Even though there are times we wish he were." She didn't seem to know how to take that remark, so I added, "He can be kind of a pain in the butt sometimes."

She swept a finger across the eyelid that was nearest me and looked back at the photograph as Dog, concerned with the tone of her voice, nudged her with his broad muzzle. "I seem to remember that."

"You know Lucian?"

She petted Dog in reassurance. "Does he live here, in town?"

I waited a moment before responding, just to be clear that she knew I knew she was not answering my questions. "He does."

"I need to see him."

Not I *want* to see him, or I'd *like* to see him, but I *need* to see him. Checking in with my ethical barometer, I glanced at Ruby—she looked puzzled but not worried, so I took a step up, leaned a shoulder against the corner of the wall, and stuffed my hands back in my jeans. "As I've said, perhaps if you tell me what this is about?"

She took a deep breath and hugged the garment bag closer to her chest, and there was that moment of silence when all the air goes out of the room. Her voice whistled with her breath again as she spoke. "I have something . . ." She looked down. "Something that I need to return to him."

2

The gentle snow was still falling as we drove the short distance to the Durant Home for Assisted Living—flurries really, adding a fresh thin layer of white onto the tired gray furrows that had been plowed to the sides of the road. The Currier & Ives scene had a Dickensian feel, with the cottonwoods frosted in white like the hard sauce on top of a plum pudding and the dirt on the side of the road reminding me that in Dickens's time, Londoners had only a gallon of clean water a week on average—drink or bathe, your choice.

As we'd come out of the office, I'd noticed the Honda with out-of-state plates parked in the guest spot. "You're from California?"

"Not originally." Her face was turned toward the passenger-side window of my unit, her words fogging the glass in bursts. "I live in San Francisco now, but I was born in Wyoming, in Powell, near Heart Mountain."

I immediately thought about the World War II internment camp that had been there and connected the slight epicanthic folds at the corners of her eyes to her heritage. "You're of Japanese ancestry?"

"A quarter. My grandmother was Japanese, and my grandfather was a rancher in Park County." She turned and looked at me. "Not too many stayed in the area after the war, but my grandfather was a guard there, and they fell in love; he used to sneak her art supplies . . ."

"Your grandmother was a painter?"

She laughed softly. "Not really."

I smiled back, turning the corner and pulling into the parking lot of the facility. "Is that how you know Lucian, through your grandfather?"

"No, I met him when I passed through here one time." She unbuckled her safety belt and clutched the bag a little closer as I put the Bullet in park. "It's also when I met you."

Before I could ask, she'd slipped from the seat and closed the door behind her. I watched as she crossed to the shoveled sidewalk, turned toward the building, and stood there with her head lowered, still with the vinyl sack hanging over her arms. The bottom of the thing turned gently in the slight breeze like an unfurled flag; whatever was in there was bulky but not long.

I piled out and opened the door for Dog, who, with the experience of countless Tuesday night chess matches, led the way, his tail raised like a question mark.

"Jingle Bells" was playing through the speaker system, a Count Basie version I remembered having heard down at the Elk Mountain Hotel when Martha and I had spent New Year's there about twenty-five years ago, before her illness. As we walked toward the front desk, I could see that Mary Jo Johnson, a member of the staff, was engaged in a heated conversation with a client about the use of one of the communal rooms, informing him that the nightly Bingo was being preempted by a local middle school holiday concert. As a matter of courtesy, I waited until the conversation was over and then signed the guestbook.

Mary Jo watched me sign my name. "The natives are restless."

I stopped in mid-dotting. "Great—what set them off?"

She sighed. "Mrs. Hayden probably isn't going to make it through the night; Doc Bloomfield is staying with her." She nodded her head toward the other wing of the building. "It's hard during the holidays, with so many of them passing."

"I'll go over later and visit with Isaac and her—I think my mother was one of Mrs. Hayden's baking buddies from church."

"Thank you, Walter." Her face stiffened. "There is one more thing." She glanced around, as if trying to keep a secret. "Lucian shot the television in the lounge."

I raised my eyes and, suddenly tired, looked at her. "Again?"

"Again."

I glanced at the young woman at my side, who was politely ignoring the conversation.

"Fox News; that's the second one in a year and now there's no holiday entertainment for the masses."

I thought about it. "Well, at least you've got the middle school musical show."

Not saying a word, she stared at me.

"I'll speak with him." I nodded, making sure she knew I was aware of the severity of the situation. "And I'll get Bert from Mossholders to get another one sent over from Sheridan."

Mary Jo studied me. "Flat screen, please."

I rested the chain-connected pen back in the holder and started down the hallway. "Merry Christmas."

She called after the three of us, "No smaller than forty-two inches."

At the far end of the hall, I raised a fist and knocked on the door. The old sheriff's hearing, having always been keen, had declined a little lately, so, after getting no response, I banged on the door again. "Lucian?"

Inside, I could hear a voice, accompanied by a thumping noise that could only be my predecessor hopping toward the door; he had most likely forgotten his prosthetic leg, so I grabbed Dog's collar—he had bowled my former boss over in his enthusiasm to get to the man's sofa on our last visit. "Is this my ribey-ass, horseshit chess partner who usually doesn't show up until the middle of the damned night?"

It was five-thirty.

The door swung open viciously, and we were treated to the sight of an old, one-legged man in boxer shorts and a wife-beater T-shirt with more than a little twenty-three-year-old Pappy Van Winkle's Family Reserve on his breath. He stared at me, then at the young woman, and then back to me, before shutting the hollow-core door in our faces.

His voice, not having lost any of its crotchetiness, carried through it. "Jesus H. Christ, you could've told me I had company."

I turned and smiled down at the woman as he continued to crash and bang around inside. "He doesn't get too many visitors."

After a few minutes, he thumped closer, and the door flung open to reveal the same man now standing there with a four-prong cane and resplendent in a vintage Pendleton wool shirt, jeans, and one polished Paul Bond boot, his bristle-brush crew-cut hair combed and pomaded.

"Where's your leg?"

He glanced around as if it might've snuck up on him at an ass-kicking contest. "Well, if I knew that I'd have the damn thing on, now wouldn't I?" He turned to look at the young woman and extended his hand, the knuckles scarred but the fingernails clean and blunt cut. "How do you do, miss."

Bashfully, she shook the proffered appendage and studied him.

They were about the same height. Lucian, unsure of the situation but with women always gracious to a fault, hopped back and invited us in, Dog of course leading the way.

His *keepers*, as he liked to refer to the people who helped him, had made their annual gesture toward holiday festooning by stringing blinking, multicolored lights outside his sliding glass doors, but there was little else to recommend the season other than a pine-scented candle that partially masked the vague but ever-present odor of pipe tobacco and Ben-Gay.

The chessboard was sitting on the side table between the two large, overstuffed leather chairs that he had brought with him from the ancestral Connally family ranch house, along with the aforementioned bourbon and a telltale glass of half-melted ice.

He gathered a *Durant Courant* and his holstered sidearm from one of the massive chairs and handed both to me, thereby discovering his prosthetic leg lying beneath. "Well, hell . . ."

Dog took up his position on the sofa, and I gestured for the woman to take a seat in the chair that had been cleaned of Lucian's paraphernalia as I assisted him in sitting in the other. He rolled up his pant leg and began strapping the prosthetic on, pointy-toed cowboy boot and all.

Slipping the newspaper under my arm and hanging the worn leather gun belt from my shoulder, I pulled out the revolver and could, indeed, smell the quartzite and gunpowder residue from when it had been fired. "Lucian, you need to stop shooting the TVs."

He licked some spittle onto his thumb and rubbed away a spot on his boot but said nothing.

"It's getting to be an expensive habit." I clicked the cylinder open on the revolver and dumped the remaining rounds into the pocket of my sheepskin coat; it was an exercise in futility until I discovered where he stashed his ammo, but it made me feel better.

He finally glanced up. "Well, are you just gonna stand there like the high cock o'laural between here and saltwater, or are you gonna offer the lady a drink?"

I sighed and turned to the young woman, who was preoccupied with staring at the wartime leaflet framed on the wall, the Japanese one that denounced the Doolittle Raid in which the old sheriff had taken part.

I looked down at the dent in the back of Lucian's head, the result of a run-in with the four Baroja brothers and a tire iron when they had taken exception to the fact that he'd eloped with their sister. It seemed like everybody in the county had attempted to beat some sense into him at some time or another, but it didn't seem that any of us had made so much as a dent, figuratively speaking.

When Lucian was fifteen, he ran away from the family ranch near Sheridan, Wyoming. Admittedly a drastic move, Lucian told me on more than one occasion that it had been the best damn decision he'd ever made, considering that the alternative would have been staring at the ass end of a couple hundred cows for the rest of his life. He had convinced the Yentzer brothers, who had owned Elkhorn Airways in Sheridan proper, to teach him to fly and let him bunk in the loft of their small Quonset hangar in return for working as a mechanic helper and hangar sweeper.

Both Dick and Jack Yentzer had been members of Lucian's original Tuesday night poker crew, but Jack had died when a cargo shift in his Piper Cub had blocked the aft control stick, causing the plane to pitch up and stall out, and Dick had been found dead in the bathroom by his family. This would not be worth telling except that as the story goes, he was found dead clutching the front of the sink and staring at himself in the mirror.

My reverie was broken by the young woman's voice as she read from the framed leaflet on the wall: " 'The cruel, inhuman, and beastlike American pilots who, in a bold intrusion of the holy territory of the Empire on April 18, 1942, dropped incendiaries and bombs on hospitals, schools, and private houses and even dive-strafed playing school-children, were captured, court-martialed, and severely punished according to military law—' "

"Miss?"

She looked up at me.

I slipped off my coat and laid it on the sofa beside Dog. "Would you like a drink?"

"I . . . Sure."

I gestured toward the bottle. "It would appear that the libation of choice at the shank of the evening is bourbon."

"I'll have bourbon." She smiled but covered it with a hand as Lucian paused in his labors to glance at her.

Nodding, I started for the abbreviated kitchen as the old sheriff went back to attending to his fourth limb. "I'll get you a fresh setup, Lucian."

Snatching his glass, I put the folded newspaper onto the counter and rested the holstered revolver on its front page, which announced that the problem with the homeless, who had been run out of the shelter in the mornings these weeks before Christmas and had subsequently occupied the library, had been solved when a local church had allowed them to stay in its cafeteria until the shelter opened again at dinner—God bless us every one.

I rinsed his glass; it took a while to find another clean one, let alone two, since I was thinking it would be a good idea to get into the holiday spirit myself. Breaking the cubes from the tray, I returned to see Lucian rerolling the cuff of his jeans back down over the initialed, handcrafted boot.

"There, like a new man." He winked at the young woman. "Or three-quarters of one."

She pointed toward the leaflet. "Is that how you lost your leg?"

"Lose hell; they cut it off . . . Course, I've been losing it ever since." He glanced back at the framed yellowed piece of paper and then shook his head. "Nope, lost it not paying attention to where Beltran Etxepare was keeping his hands."

I arrived with the glasses, and she shifted her eyes to me. "Basque bootleggers."

Her eyes widened. "Oh."

He snatched the bottle from the table and motioned for me to set the glasses on it. "I'll pour; I know how liberal you can be." He tipped the bottle into the three tumblers, and I noticed he held out the lightest to me.

I took the Lismore Waterford tumbler—my mother had had the same design—leaned against the substantial wing of his cowhide chair, and gestured toward the young woman, who sniffed the spirits, made a face, and then held the cut-glass like a benediction, the reflection from the golden liquid underlighting her face, making the scar more evident in that small illumination—white and ghostlike.

"This lady says she knows you, Lucian."

He motioned toward the vinyl garment bag, still in her lap. "Well, I didn't figure she was from the dry cleaners." He winked at her. "No tickee, no shirtee?"

There was an uncomfortable silence as I listened to the ticking of the clock on Lucian's sideboard and made a conscious effort to melt into the floor.

Finally, she spoke. "I'm Japanese, not Chinese."

He sipped the Pappy Van Winkle's and studied her. "And I'm confused; if you don't mind my asking, just who the hell are you, anyway?"

With her black hair shrouding her face, she could have been one of Henry Standing Bear's many unofficial nieces as she moved a few of the chess pieces with the tips of her fingers. With her head still down, she carefully set the glass on the coaster beside the board and took a quick breath to steady herself. "You don't remember me, either."

The old sheriff craned his neck to look up at me and then back to her. "You'll have to forgive me, young lady, but my memory isn't quite what it used to be. Perhaps if you were to give me a clue?"

Her face came up, and the glow from the blinking lights challenged the reflection from the tumbler and planed the scar again as if lightning had struck across her forehead.

Her perfect lips moved, and the whistle returned in her breath. *"Steamboat."*

December 24, 1988

The fire trucks' emergency lights rhythmically crashed into the plate glass of the observation deck along with a few snowflakes that flew toward my face and then against the outside of the window, the ones that missed the glass avoiding the Durant terminal altogether in a race for Nebraska. I studied the line I'd read over and over again in my attempts at distracting myself: ". . . no space of regret can make amends for one life's opportunity misused. . . ."

I stuffed the leather-bound copy of *A Christmas Carol* into the inside pocket of my sheepskin coat and pulled at the brim of my new hat. With a little help from Martha, my daughter, Cady, who had turned nine in April, had given me a very nice chocolate brown one as an early Christmas present. I adjusted the brim, rested my gloved hand against the window, and stared into the wind coming from the Bighorn Mountains to the west.

What would Lucian Connally, the sheriff who had lost to me in the election in November, have done?

I felt someone standing beside me and glanced over to see the Ferg, peering in the same direction, his voice raised to be heard above the wind, pressing against the glass in repetitive howls, almost as if the noise and the revolving yellow lights represented the sound and its accompanying fury. "Weren't they supposed to be here already?"

I turned and looked at the moonfaced man, roughly my age, and the one I'd leapfrogged to sheriff only two months ago—a move that didn't seem so smart right now. "Yep."

"The NOAA says it's shaping up to be the worst storm of the century, and it's headed our way."

I took a deep breath and slowly exhaled, hazing the glass in front of my face. "The old-timers say forty-nine was horrible, but I don't remember it . . . You?"

He shook his head. "Can't say I do." He turned back to the darkness. "What the heck are you gonna do, Walt?"

I tipped my hat back, smoothed my mustache, and leaned a forearm against the window, hoping that maybe if I got those ten inches closer, I would see the running lights of a Flight For Life helicopter out of Billings. "Funny, I was just thinking about that."

"Only one survivor?"

I listened to the wind press against the casings with that scrubbing sound it can make, hoping it wasn't attempting to clean the helicopter from the sky. "Yep."

"How bad?"

"Burns." I sighed, thinking how it was the one thing you

didn't want to say when talking about a child. "Fifteen percent TBSA's with inhalation injuries." Total Body Surface Area burns over 5 percent were bad enough to cause most doctors to want to get a patient to a pediatric ICU as quickly as possible, but with the added complications of smoke inhalation injuring airway tissues, this little girl needed Colorado, and she needed it within hours or she would die. "Bad enough that they couldn't do anything in Billings; bad enough that the only chance is Children's Hospital in Denver."

Another reflection—Isaac Bloomfield, the doctor I'd called in to help the traveling medical staff who would be with the victim, was standing just behind us holding a sheaf of papers in his shaking hands. "Walt?"

"Yep."

"Emma at the administrative office says that since the gusts are approaching forty miles an hour they had to alter their flight plan; they're still thirty minutes away."

"Right."

"I thought you would want to know."

"I do." I calculated in my head as my hand curled into a fist. "Any idea where Rick Koehmstedt is?"

"In the hangar with Julie."

I had known of Julie Luehrman—she had taught part-time at Cady's school—but I had finally actually met her six months ago while waiting for a chartered flight carrying the attorney general. I'd been eavesdropping, listening to her explain the finer points of plotting, bearing, and distance to one of her student pilots. "Thanks, Doc."

I pushed off and walked between the two men, the Ferg slipping a hand to my shoulder. "Walt, it would take eight hours to drive it in these conditions, and the Highway Patrol has already pulled the barricades down."

I nodded and continued on.

The main hangar of the Durant Airport was only ten yards from the terminal, but with the wind and the snow piled from the storm that had hit a couple of days ago, it might as well have been a hundred. I cranked my hat down as far as it would go, flipped up the collar of my coat, forced the door open, and, tacking to my right to counter the pressure of the wind, trudged along the snow-clogged chain-link fence. There was no chance of my thoughts being blown away—they clung to me like the bony fist of Christmas Future.

There had been an automobile crash on I-90 where it merged with I-94 on the outskirts of Billings, Montana. There was a fire, and three people were dead; the one person who had survived would not continue to do so unless I figured out a way to get her to Denver. When the high-powered helicopter had left Billings they'd thought they had a chance of outrunning the Canadian front that was barreling down out of Alberta, but conditions had changed and now the authorities were shutting down the highways and pilots were grounding anything that flew north and west of here other than a few wayward Canada geese.

I stumbled against the door of the hangar and grabbed at the handle, forcing it open just enough to let my bulk through. A large clump of snow slid from the roof and landed squarely on top of my new hat. Standing there for a moment, I took a breath of the heated air and could smell the tang of fresh paint and the sound of a drill somewhere in the depths of the maintenance hangar.

As I walked past the administrative office and down the hallway, I shook my hat against my leg and stopped long enough to get an indication of where the sound was coming from within the enormous building. As I looked around, I noticed that there was a large aeronautical chart pinned to the wall that had expanding graduated circles drawn around the Durant Airport like a bull's-eye.

A long, narrow, tape-like string marked in ten-mile increments was attached to the chart with a nail on Durant as a center point. I grabbed the end of it in my wet fingers and stretched it out along a path directly to Denver, noting the reading—28.5 tick marks, 150 degrees at 285 miles as the crow flies.

The overhead heaters blasted in an attempt to keep the temperature in the tin building over fifty degrees. I could still see my breath as I headed in and ducked under the wing of a Cessna, around the tail of an old Navion, past the fuselages of a Maule and a vintage Beechcraft, and around the engine of another much larger plane that overshadowed the entire rear of the hangar.

Rick was the airport manager and was watching as his friend and protégé, wearing an elastic headlamp over her ball cap, drilled holes in an angular piece of aluminum. He pointed to a spot on the metal where Julie was to drill the next hole, and even with the vague scent of high-octane aviation fuel in the air, the ever-present cigar hung from the young man's lip. Julie shook her head, and the now full-time hangar rat smiled as I approached the rolling worktable. "Fat pilots—over time they bend the seat rails."

"Then I shouldn't fly."

"You haven't got any fat on you."

"I have tendencies—vitamin R—otherwise known as Rainier beer."

Julie smiled and Rick snorted and pointed at me with his cigar. "From what I heard, you don't like flying, period."

"I don't—especially helicopters and especially since Vietnam; besides, I barely have enough fingers on one hand to count how many times I've been out with the Durant search and rescue team looking for a crashed helicopter."

"Then what are you doin' at an airport?"

"Waiting on a helicopter."

"Yeah, I heard." He laughed and leaned both elbows on the rolling cart, causing it to move; Julie gave him a dirty look. "Hell, those eggbeaters are twice as dangerous as a fixed wing." He smirked at her. "They have thousands of moving parts and are prone to behaving badly. When the rotors quit, watch those chopper pilots really start to sweat."

"What are the chances of this crew getting refueled and heading on down to Colorado?"

"None." He stabbed the cigar back in the corner of his mouth as if it were a dart on a corkboard. "The runways at Denver Stapleton are open but fighting drifting snow and Chinook winds. Julie and I checked the forecast and the SIGMET/AIRMETs at Sheridan Flight Service, and in a little over an hour that front is going to hit and there isn't anything going to fly—not even Santa Claus."

"The medevac can't outrun it?"

Koehmstedt guffawed around his cheroot. "It's a fast-moving cold front coming from the northwest. Even if they get out of here before the front really hits Durant, it will move in from the west and block the chopper's route south of here toward Denver. At best, that thing they're coming in on will do a hundred and thirty, maybe a bit better with a tailwind, sure not fast enough to get far enough south before the front blocks its path."

With her free hand Julie tipped her bright yellow Pilot Cub cap back and plucked off her safety glasses, revealing a set of ferocious, blue-yonder eyes. "Helicopters are actually better in most rescue situations because they're more maneuverable, but they're not good in high winds and they don't handle icing well." Julie waved the drill in my direction. "Can't compete with a fixed wing in speed, either."

I glanced around the hangar. "Do we have anything here that'll make it?"

Rick laughed. "Not only no, but hell no."

Julie set the drill down, switched off the headlamp, and stuffed the safety glasses in the front pocket of her blue Carhartt coveralls. "A pilot flying these little guys would lose control and get ripped apart in those conditions, Walt." She studied the small planes and then shook her head. "Most of these can't go as fast as the chopper anyway; besides, where are you going to put the gurney, equipment, and medical staff?"

I could feel my breath getting shorter as my options ran out, and I leaned against the back of the propeller of the plane that overshadowed us. I slipped a little, looked down, and noticed that I was standing in a puddle of oil that must have originated from the big plane's engine exhaust stack. First my hat and now my boots. Quickly stepping aside, I looked up at the stained surface of the plane, a dulled silver, with rust that elicited little confidence. "What about this one?"

They both shook their heads, Rick the first to speak. "Oh, Sheriff, you're really grabbing at straws. This is an old VB-25J VIP transport that was Eisenhower's private plane during the D-Day invasion. It ended up in the boneyard at Davis-Monthan Air Force Base in Arizona and was sold as surplus."

"How'd it get here?"

Pushing the rolling cart back in Rick's direction, Julie shimmied to the side. "A company out of Tucson bought it to use for grasshopper and sagebrush spray contracts along the foot of the Bighorns and on into Nebraska, but it had leaky hydraulics."

Julie moved closer, placing a hand on the landing gear. "The company tried to fix her, but on one trip it had a serious hydraulic failure and the pilot landed here. The plane ran off the edge of the runway, plowing grass and tumbleweeds, finally coming to a stop after damaging her nosewheel."

Rick tossed a dirty rag onto the cart and picked out a clean one. "The contracts fell through, the company went out of business, and the plane was abandoned. After a few years the county sold it to Hawkins/Powers out of Greybull to use for slurry bombing forest fires."

Rick looked over at me rubbing the soles of my boots on the concrete. "They're good guys—even hired Julie last season as a copilot." Rick offered me the clean rag. "Takes guts to hire a woman in this business."

Julie shrugged. "They had the old spray tank removed from the bomb bay so they can put in one of their new light-weight designs, but the original doors are still there. We fixed the nosewheel, even cleaned the bird's nests out of the air intakes so I think the heaters work. The leaky hydraulic valves still need fixed, but the fuel tanks are solid as long as you don't fill them over four hundred fifty gallons."

I glanced up at the large plane. "What happens if you put more than four hundred and fifty gallons in it?"

"She leaks fuel like a cow pissing on a flat rock." Rick took some matches out of his pocket and tried to relight his cigar. "The ole bird is stuck here till somebody can come over and fly her out."

I began studying the antique, unable to give up my last straw. "How fast is it?"

Rick drew his face back as if I'd smacked him. "Close to three hundred miles an hour, but like she said, the hydraulics are shot and there isn't anybody to fly her."

I turned to Julie. "You're a pilot, right?"

She shook her head. "I'm not type rated in something like this. I mean I got checked out as a copilot and have my commercial certificate with one hundred hours—two hundred and fifty in various single engines as a flight instructor—but nothing like this. It takes an incredible amount of training and hours to get certified on a plane this size, Walt."

I stepped back and ran my eyes over the lines of the thing, taking in the twin engines, the faded air force insignia, and the massive width of the wingspan. "What are the chances that the pilot of the helicopter might be able to fly it?"

"None." Rick's turn to shake his head. "Hell, nobody this side of the Bighorns flies these things anymore; they're antiques."

I continued to look at the beast, and as I stood there with my hands in my pockets, I tipped my hat back and studied the numbers on the side of one of the tail fins—34030. My eyes played across the length of the thing, its aerodynamics and sheer bulk making it appear like a whale shark swimming with guppies. I walked closer and noticed the unusual nose art—a bucking horse and rider in faded brown and gold, the name spiraled across the side. "Why does this plane look familiar?"

Rick drew in on his cigar and blew smoke under the wide wings. "It's a VB-25J, a transport version of the old Mitchell B-25s—you know, one of the most used bombers of the Second World War—but I'm telling you, other than maybe the crews over in Greybull, nobody in these parts can fly the damn thing.

I pulled at my sideburns and continued staring at the plane as thoughts crazier than the wild Wyoming wind whipping the outside of the hangar crashed against the insides of my skull.

"I know somebody who can."

4

The Euskadi Bar in downtown Durant was the place where I'd first been offered the job as deputy, and the man who had hired me still frequented the place. Lucian Connally was a shrewd poker player who rarely lost and was sitting at a card table in his favorite chair with a large stack of chips in front of him. During his time as sheriff, he kept his games at the Euskadi low stakes and friendly, but on a few occasions he would put someone in charge of the office and take a sabbatical, as he was fond of saying, spending a day or two playing high-stakes poker in a casino across either the Montana or South Dakota lines.

The three other men at the table tonight—Tom Koltiska, Gerald Holman, and John Buell—turned to look at the Ferg and me as we came through the door. Lucian paused, his Old Rip Van Winkle bourbon in midair. "Well, looky here, if it ain't Frick and Frack—you boys run out of crosswalks?"

I slapped the glass out of his hand, sending it and the expensive bourbon tumbling across the table's felted surface.

"Jesus H. Christ!"

"How many of those have you had?"

He made a face. "Two."

I reached across the bar and grabbed Jerry Aranzadi, the Basque bartender, by his shirtfront. "How many?"

"Three, he's had three."

I swiveled my face around and the brims of our hats met. "Can you fly?"

Now he really looked confused, at least I hoped that's what it was. "What?"

"Can you fly? I've got a Flight For Life chopper coming in from Billings, and I need somebody to outrun this storm and fly them the rest of the way to Denver."

He looked past me and studied the blowing snow outside the warm glow of the bar. "In this crap, you've got to be joking."

"I'm not."

He stared past me at the whistling snow shooting past the plate-glass windows like miniature banshees doing drive-bys in search of souls. He shook his head. "Can't be done."

I looked back at Jerry, remembering I still had hold of him. "Have you got any coffee?"

"Yes."

I turned to the Ferg. "Get my thermos out of my truck, would you?" He did as I said while the bartender grabbed a mug and the pot from the burner on the bar back and poured Lucian a jolt of joe. "The chopper will be here in twenty minutes with a girl in it—a little girl that's burned and won't survive the night without transport to Denver. They're fueling and getting the plane ready as we speak."

"What kind of plane? You can't fly just anything in this stuff."

I smiled down at him. "Trust me, I found you one."

The old sheriff downed almost half the coffee in one gulp. "Anybody checked the weather along the way or filed a flight plan so we can pick up a clearance with Salt Lake?"

"Denver, not Salt Lake."

His mouth stiffened. "Till you get nearly past the VOR at Crazy Woman, you're still going to be under the auspices of Salt Lake air traffic control center, then Denver—so I'll ask again, has anybody filed a flight plan?"

"I don't know."

He slugged down the rest of his coffee and slammed the mug on the table. "For the sheriff of this damn county, you sure don't seem to know a lot."

"What's a VOR?"

He shook his head. "Very high frequency Omnidirectional Range, a two-phase 360-degree signal by which you navigate the damn plane." He shook his head and repeated. "You sure as hell don't know much."

The Ferg reappeared with my Stanley thermos, the one that Martha had given me for my birthday with a sticker that Cady had cut out that read DRINKING FUEL in capital letters, and Jerry Aranzadi immediately began filling it. I dragged Lucian up by the shoulders and started him toward the door. "I do know I've got to cut you off and get you in the air, flyboy."

By the time we got back up to the airport the chopper had landed, and Rick and Julie were rapidly transferring the patient into the relative warmth of the hangar along with an EMT and the victim's grandmother.

Isaac Bloomfield was speaking with both of them while

Rick conferred with the helicopter pilot by the door. We stormed past and then turned to look at the pale man in the jumpsuit, his hands firmly planted in his underarms. "No way, we barely got in here with our lives; anybody that goes back up in this is looking to be spread from here to Omaha in pieces no bigger than a quarter."

I swung around and faced him. "Are you certified on a multiengine?"

He looked up at me, his eyes flashing the defiance of the fearful. "No, I'm not." He was still sweating from the exertion of the flight. "And even if I was, I wouldn't be going up in these conditions." He ran a hand through his thick hair. "I'm telling you, people are going to die if you try it."

I glanced at the small, intubated body on the ventilated gurney as they wheeled it underneath the bomber. "Well, I know for sure that one of us will if we don't."

Isaac joined the Ferg and me as Lucian wandered to our left, deftly sidestepping the puddle of engine oil that had dripped from the large plane's exhaust stacks and had shanghaied me earlier. "The grandmother indicated to me that she's willing to try it." The doc gestured toward the unmoving man by the doorway. "But the EMT keeps talking about insurance and says he'll only go if the helicopter pilot does."

I glanced at the man, giving him just one more chance. "Please."

His head dropped, and he looked at his folded arms. "I told you, I don't know how to fly that thing; it should be in a museum or a scrap yard somewhere." He shook his head, steadfast. "You guys aren't pilots, so you don't know; we barely made it in here with our lives and it's doing nothing but getting worse. Nobody in their right mind would fly in this weather."

I glanced behind me at the short man who was standing under the wing and drinking a second mug of coffee, his eyes running over the sleek lines of the medium bomber like a long-lost lover. "You could be right."

I walked over to the spot where my old boss, the man whose job I'd taken only a few months earlier, albeit with his approval, stood under the shadow of the vintage aircraft.

I could only imagine the things that must've been racing through his head. Things like April 18, 1942, when he and fifteen other pilots had lifted the spirits of an almost defeated nation by flying this selfsame aircraft off of the heaving deck of the USS *Hornet*, or being spotted by a Japanese fishing vessel that forced them to accomplish this daredevil feat 170 miles early, about fuel exhaustion and stormy nighttime conditions with zero visibility.

Lucian had continued to fly as a civilian, working part time on short contracts around the region, off and on over the years after World War II. After losing his leg he was able to regain his medical certificate through something he called a waiver, which simply required him to use an artificial limb. He'd take vacations to go fly and every so often he'd call me in to cover so he could just take off, but I had no idea how long it had been since he'd flown an aircraft like *Steamboat*.

I became aware of his lips moving. "Old airplanes never die; they just get handed over to the Air Transport Group, fly a while, go to surplus, and then get sold to those aerial fire-fighters in Greybull." He held his mug out, and I unscrewed the top of the thermos and refilled it for him as he took a step forward, his dark eye like a black widow suspended in the web of wrinkles at the corner of the socket—just as dark and just as deadly. His matinee profile was still sharp and chiseled as he raised the mug, the steam filming his glasses like high-altitude cloud cover.

He held the mug there, stopping just short of his lips as he read the scripted letters on the side of the craft. "Well, hello *Steamboat . . ."*

5

"What do you think you're doing?"

Julie held a gallon jug of water, or what I assumed was water, rattling with ice, and tossed her flight bag and a back-pack up into the nose of *Steamboat*. Throwing a thumb over her shoulder to where Lucian was fiddling with one of the combination locks on a locker in the hallway, Julie smiled. "He's only got one leg, so you're going to need a copilot."

"I thought you weren't certified for this thing."

Stuffing her ash-blond hair up under her cap and donning a pair of black horn-rims, she set the plastic container on the ladder and zipped up the front of her overalls. "Not as a captain, but last summer I got some flight time in as a copilot, and I have both my legs, so I'm all you've got."

I was surrounded by crazy people. "As I recall, they're nice legs."

"Flatterer." She glanced over my shoulder to look back at the old Doolittle Raider and put on a padded jacket; she pulled out a pack of Beemans chewing gum and offered me a stick. "Just do me a favor?"

I declined the gum. "What's that?"

She unwrapped it, popped it in her mouth, and smiled a dazzling grin. "Get him to stop calling me Toots."

I listened as the wind buckled and popped against the steel siding of the hangar. "You don't have to do this."

"Look who's talking." She grabbed a notebook. "Walt, I at least know what kinds of conditions we're up against, and I don't get flight sick like some people I know. I think you're the one who needs to not do this." She studied me. "Have you called Martha?"

"Not yet." I started to turn but then pointed at the gallon jug. "What's that for?"

She smiled. "My mouth gets dry when I get nervous, and I've got a sneaking suspicion I'm going to be getting nervous on this flight, so I'm taking my water and my Beemans. I'm betting I'll finish both by the time this flight is over." She put the gum back in her pocket, picked up the jug, and reached into the fuselage. Placing a foot on the ladder, she disappeared, her voice the only thing reaching me. "Stay here, Walt."

As I turned toward the administrative offices, Lucian started banging on the door of the locker. I paused long enough to ask, "What are you doing, old man?"

He turned the dial again, tried the latch, and started over. "This is my locker—I've had it since after the war—and I still keep a pair of headphones, a flight bag, and a few other things in here." He yanked on the handle, and the door opened. "8-6-45, the date we dropped the big one—knew I wouldn't forget that."

I looked at him strangely, but he ignored me. "Okay, but

they've about got that thing ready to run, so we need to shake a leg." He glanced at me. "No pun intended."

He continued to gather his things and disregarded me, so I ducked in the office to take care of my last-minute business. The phone was an old rotary, and I quickly dialed 6798, my home number.

Martha picked up on the first ring, and her voice sounded tired and sexy but maybe that was just me, wanting to go home and be in bed with her, not here with a bunch of cantankerous pilots. "Where are you?"

"I'm at the airport."

She sighed. "What airport?"

"Our airport, Durant."

"You hate to fly. Why are you there?"

"There was an accident up in Montana, and there's a victim who needs to be flown down to Denver."

Her voice was wary. "Tonight?"

"Yep." I listened to the silence on the line and thought about how many nights she'd gotten calls similar to this one and how many more nights she would.

When I'd gotten back from being a Marine investigator in Vietnam, I'd sworn I'd never make a living behind a badge again, but the only available job had been as a deputy in the Absaroka County Sheriff's Department. We needed the money, and I'd taken it. A decade and a half later, here I was, the sheriff of the county but only because Lucian Connally had wanted to retire and there was a pay raise—neither my wife nor I were completely satisfied with the situation.

The strain in her voice was becoming more evident. "You're going to fly down there with the medevac crew?"

"Not exactly." I explained the situation quickly, so that

she couldn't interrupt and inject some sanity into the conversation, but I finally finished and there was nothing more for me to say.

She, on the other hand, was not at a loss for words. "Oh, Walt. Is it safe?"

This is the point when, if you are given to fabrication, a deceiving man would lie, but I knew that if I were to be scattered across the high plains in pieces no bigger than pocket change, I probably needed to tell the truth, mostly. "I guess." I glanced back through the open doorway and watched as Rick beat on the plane's bomb-bay doors with a rubber mallet in an attempt to get them closed. "Everybody seems to think so."

"Walter, it's Christmas Eve. Cady is counting on you being here in the morning."

"I know, I know . . ." I continued to watch as Isaac Bloomfield, one of the techs, and Julie carefully lifted the covered gurney with the portable ventilator, battery pack, and oxygen tanks into the main body of the old bomber at midships, just behind the bomb-bay doors, the grandmother following, tears on her cheeks. I cupped the receiver close to my mouth. "It's a child; a little girl."

Her voice grew small. "There's no other way?"

"No." I listened again to the wind in the wires. "Martha, what if it was our daughter; what if it was Cady?"

She didn't answer right away, but when she did, her voice had softened. "All right, you go, but you make sure you're back here safe for Christmas. That nine-year-old daughter of yours is asleep in the next room, and she's been attempting to read *To Kill a Mockingbird* and talking about law school again."

"So, she'll be the greatest-legal-mind-of-our-time." I sighed, joking. "What'd we do wrong?"

"I blame Henry."

I smiled at the mention of our good friend and operator of the Red Pony Bar out near the Northern Cheyenne Reservation and wished that the Bear were here now, if for no other reason than for good medicine.

"Get going, Sheriff, I've got a feeling we're going to be paying for tuition for the rest of our lives."

I tucked the receiver in close, imagining she could feel my proximity. "Good thing we've got a long road ahead of us, huh?"

A trace of emotion slipped into her voice. "I love you."

6

I poked my head up into the fuselage and glanced back into the moderate darkness of the plane's interior, where Isaac and the med-tech were attaching the gurney to the bracings on the floor, the IVs and battery pack hanging from the rounded ceiling of the bomber, giving the appearance that the victim had become part of the two-engine aircraft; her grandmother, covered in blankets, sat on a jump seat. I yelled to Isaac, a concentration camp survivor who had been the general medical practitioner for the greater Durant, Wyoming, region for thirtysome years, the man who had delivered Cady and took care of all of us. "You better get out of there, Doc, and head home. Sky King is getting ready to fire this baby up, so wish us luck—I think we might need it."

Isaac approached the hatch and kneeled down to talk to me, his heavily padded down coat bunching around his face. "Sky King?"

"Didn't you ever watch television, Doc?"

"Very little." He straightened the knit cap on his head,

which read MEADOWLARK SKI RESORT, and looked me in the eye. "It looks like you get me, Walter."

I glanced at the young man who had flown in on the helicopter from Billings. "He's not going?"

"No, so I am."

I lowered my voice. "Isaac, are you crazy?"

He kneeled in closer, and I could see his hands still shaking. "I am not crazy, and as a matter of fact, I'm profoundly scared." He smiled a timid smile, one that wouldn't hold. "She'll need someone to check the battery pack on the ventilator and possibly change the oxygen tanks and IVs. She'll need a doctor, Walter. I have a suspicion that she's suffering from a pneumothorax . . ."

I climbed up into the bomber. "English, Doc."

He pulled some X-rays from a thick manila envelope and held one up to the opaque light of the side-gunner window, pointing at a small mark within the girl's chest. "Possible air trapped between the lungs where they were punctured by rib fractures."

I covered my face with a hand. "You've got to be kidding."

He pulled out his stethoscope and listened to her breathing.

"It could be the case, that or the whistling in her breathing is due to smoke inhalation and damage by fire and steam. Hot smoke usually burns only the pharynx, but steam can burn the airway below the glottis."

I peeked at him through my fingers. "So, what are we supposed to do if it's the pneumo-whatever-it-is?"

"Well, we should be able to drain the pressure with a regular needle from a large syringe, but in a worst-case scenario we will have to open her up and drain the air and blood from the cavity in her chest."

"On the plane?"

He glanced behind him and lowered his voice. "It's only a one- to two-centimeter incision . . . At any rate, Walter, you need medical expertise, and I am what you have."

I looked around. "Have we got the equipment to do all that?"

"Hopefully . . ."

"Hopefully?"

"When I spoke with the surgeon, Carlton, in Billings, he was rushed, but said he had only a suspicion, that there hadn't been enough time to do a thorough examination and the radiologist might not have had time to review the X-rays. Carlton threw in some equipment, just in case, but I'm in hopes that we won't have to use it." He shook his head. "This is nothing in comparison to the burns, Walter, I can't treat her for that in Durant. As limited as our abilities might be between here and Denver, she'll die if we don't take this foolish flight."

I tried to smile back, but mine wasn't sticking either. "Foolish flight, huh? Maybe we should paint that on the side of old *Steamboat*." I looked behind me at another bulkhead that seemed to restrict access to the front of the plane. "How do you get up to the cockpit in this thing?"

He glanced past me. "Lucian said there is a crawlspace above the bomb bay and that there are radio headsets scattered throughout the aircraft so that the crew can stay in communication with each other." He glanced toward the rear of the cabin where the burned child lay in the tented gurney, her grandmother having moved next to her to hold her hand once the med-tech had gotten out of the way. "Walter, I think someone needs to speak to Mrs. Oda about the situation."

Preoccupied with the thought of an in-flight surgical procedure, I glanced at the doc. "Who?"

"The grandmother. Mrs. Oda."

I whispered. "Why is that?"

"Because as far as I know, no one has."

I studied the older woman for a moment and thought about how little time we had as the technician continued to secure all the equipment so that it wouldn't shift in flight. Bringing my mouth down to the doc's ear, I whispered, "Didn't she say she wanted to be here to do this?"

"She indicated to me that she wants to save her grandchild, but I don't think she understands the implications of what we're doing or how dangerous it most likely will be."

I nodded. "You want me to level with her then?"

He gripped my shoulder and looked at me in honest horror. "Oh, God, no."

"Then what?"

"I don't think she speaks that much English." He paused and looked around. "That woman has just lost her sister, her son-in-law, and her daughter in a terrible crash, and I think she needs to be reassured. Someone needs to comfort her, Walter."

"I don't speak Japanese, Doc."

"Does Lucian? I mean, he was in that prison camp."

The thought of Lucian bearing the responsibility of reassuring anybody was funny under any circumstance other than this one. "Just curse words, and I don't think that's going to help."

"Well, I think that if somebody would just communicate

with her in a reassuring tone it would make her feel better, and you are the sheriff now."

"Boy howdy." I took a deep breath and then patted the doc on the arm and moved past him and the med-tech toward the tiny woman crouched by her granddaughter, the girl who was possibly the only surviving member of her immediate family. "Mrs. Oda?"

She turned her face to me as I crouched down beside her, and I was surprised at the calm there; her eyes were red-rimmed, but her features were composed as she gazed up at me. *"Hai?"*

"Mrs. Oda, I just wanted to tell you that, umm . . . that if there was any other way . . ." I shot a glance over my shoulder to the doc, who raised an eyebrow. "Umm . . ." I turned back to the woman and smiled. "Mrs. Oda, this plane may not look like much, but it's very powerful and we've got a top-notch pilot up there who is going to bore a hole in the sky getting your granddaughter down to Denver." She continued to stare at me, and I felt words unready for speech falling from my mouth. "The plane, umm . . . It's got a very lucky name—Steamboat was one of the toughest bucking horses in the history of rodeo." She continued to look at me blankly. "He's on all the license plates . . ." I sighed and leaned against the gurney. "Mrs. Oda, I don't know what to say to you, other than we're all going to do our best to get your granddaughter to Denver; I honestly don't know if this plane is tough or lucky, but I can promise you that we're willing to gamble everything, even our own lives, to save your granddaughter."

She studied me and then took my hand in hers, joining it with the other to hold the fingers of the girl; through the plastic, I looked at the child's damaged face, half covered in bandages. If not for my rib cage, I'm pretty sure my heart would've fallen out onto the floor's wire grating, but instead, as I crouched there looking at that broken face, I could feel the thing thumping in my chest.

"Amaterasu."

I glanced at her and then at the child again. "Her name is Amaterasu?"

"*Hai.*" She nodded and then gestured upward with her hands. "*Ama . . .*" She gestured again, I supposed wanting me to guess the name's meaning.

"Up? Ama—her name means up?"

The older woman shook her head and gestured even farther. "*Ama.*"

"The sky?" Her hands continued to push higher, gesturing past what I assumed meant the sky. "Heaven, you mean heaven?"

She nodded, her hands dropping, and she extended an index finger pointing at the sparkle of light on the star pinned to my chest. "*Terasu.*"

"Star?"

The older woman's fingers splayed out in a burst.

"Glow?"

She began nodding. "Amaterasu."

"Her name means shining over heaven."

I turned and looked at the med-tech as he finished up and stood, still avoiding looking at all of us. "Her name, Amaterasu, means shining over heaven—one of the doctors at St. Vincent, Frank Carlton, speaks some Japanese, and he said her name was of mythological derivation for the sun goddess who rules the heavens."

I smiled and turned back to the grandmother. "Well,

speaking of good luck—there's no way the sky can reject the sun goddess who rules the heavens."

She smiled back as I lifted her and sat her in the seat beside the gurney. Attaching a harness around her, I gestured that she should stay. "You'll be safer here, and the ride is bound to get bumpy."

As I turned, the technician was pulling up blankets and insulated coveralls through the hatch below. I took his load and distributed the heavy clothes among the three of us. "How cold is it going to get?"

The tech shook his head. "Cold, believe me; we were in a sealed cabin and we almost froze our asses off." He glanced around. "This thing isn't pressurized, is it? Does it even have heat? It's going to get cold, according to how high he flies this thing, but I'd say fifty below zero, easy."

I glanced at the gurney.

He shook his head. "She'll be fine; we've got oxygen and heat keeping her at a constant. It's you guys I'd worry about."

"Julie said she thinks the heat works." I leaned in close. "C'mon, make the flight with us."

His mouth stiffened. "No way; I've been up there and this is pure trolleyism."

"What?"

"Trolleyism. If you had this little girl on a track with a trolley bearing down on her and you could throw a switch that sent the car onto another track with five other people on it—would you throw that lever?"

"It's not the same."

His eyes studied the padded surface of the plane's interior. "You're right, because you're not even going to be able to save the girl. You're all going to die up there." His eyes came back to mine. "You're sacrificing five people's lives for the possibility of saving one girl . . ."

"It's not a question of numbers, it's a question of what you have to do, what you have to live with if you don't." I thought about the book in my pocket, the advice that the Ghost of Christmas Present gives Scrooge on decreasing the surplus population, and mumbled to myself: "Will you decide what men shall live, what men shall die? It may be that in the sight of Heaven, you are more worthless . . . [than] . . . this poor . . . child. . . ."

"Excuse me?"

His eyes were on mine when I reached out and clamped a hand on his shoulder. "Once we take off, I'm sure we'll all be fighting to save everyone's lives on board."

He shook his head and looked at the ground outside the hatchway. "Your odds are lousy."

I threw a thumb back to the tented gurney. "C'mon, we've got the sun goddess who rules the heavens; what could go wrong?"

He froze just for that instant and I thought I'd convinced him, but he shook his head some more. "No way, Sheriff; you're on your own." He stuck out a hand. "Good luck. You're going to need it."

I took a deep breath and turned to assist the doc by pulling the coveralls over his shoulders, zipping him up, and holding his down jacket for him to crawl back into.

Isaac watched as the young man exited the aircraft. "I am concerned with the sense of service in the younger generation." He adjusted the thick lenses of his glasses. "As for my generation . . ." He straightened his stocking cap as he turned to regard me. "Am I correct in the assumption that Lucian has been drinking?"

"Just enough to limber him up."

"*Mein Gott.*"

I smiled at the doc's tendency to revert back to his native language in times of duress. "Yours or mine?"

He reached out and placed a hand along the riveted frame bracing, the chromate green structure looking for all the world like the inside of a rib cage. "Anyone who will answer, Walter. Anyone who will answer."

I moved aside so that the doc could slide by and then folded my own pair of coveralls under my arm and lowered myself through the hatch and down the short ladder. "Amen to that, Doc. Amen to that."

I ducked my head and watched as the airport manager slid the ladder up, closed the doors behind me, and, twisting the latch, locked them.

Julie was standing next to him at the back hatch. "The flight plan is filed with the Sheridan Flight Service, Rick, and I entered LIFEGUARD in the remarks section since we are on a mission of an urgent medical nature and will, I'm betting, need expeditious handling—especially with this weather and this aircraft. I placed our clearance on request, but haven't gotten it yet. Can you call them back, copy it down, and read it to us over your UNICOM before we take off? We can't raise them on the ground with ours—we filed under the call sign Raider N4030LC."

"Sure, consider it done." Rick turned and motioned toward the front. "If you guys're getting on this thing, you better hustle it up; Lucian's already gone through the walk around and preflight planning." He turned back and looked at me, suddenly grim. "I double-checked the weather—they said you are crazy to do this, that there are a couple of aircraft reported down in the mountains northwest of here already . . . nobody can get to them . . . temperatures are dropping, just killer winds and blowing snow."

"Thank them for the vote of confidence." I saluted. "Killer winds and blowing snow. Roger that."

"Don't try and fool me—Marines don't fly."

"No. We crawl, generally; we're smart that way."

Looking toward the front of the hangar, I could see the Ferg and the medical tech getting ready to open the two large sliding doors so we could get the big plane out. The helicopter crew had already moved the small airplanes outside and had securely tied them down, so the hangar was pretty much empty except for *Steamboat*. As we moved past her bomb-bay doors, I smiled. "Were you just doing some modification to these?"

Rick shook his head. "The hydraulics on this piece of shit continue to leak, and one of the draws to the system are these big doors. Over time they drop, then get hung up, and you can't get them back in place without hitting 'em a few times to get 'em loose."

I unzipped the legs of the insulated coveralls he had given me and began slipping them on. "What if that happens while we're in flight?"

"Oh, if the main engine pumps go out there's a manual lever up in the cockpit on the floor between the seats that'll pressurize the system, and I've got a sneaking suspicion that that's what you're going to be doing all the way down to Colorado—pumping that handle." He reached up and patted my shoulder as I straightened the coveralls and shrugged into my sheepskin coat. "But you're a big boy, you can handle it."

I glanced at the doors, noting the space and how they didn't seem to match properly. "But really, what if they do drop?"

"Well, there's the nose-gear tow bar in there; it's about six feet long and you could use it to bang on 'em till they engage, but you're gonna be a couple thousand feet in the air, and even you're not tall enough for that. Hell, the engines or the electrical systems'll give out in this crate long before that anyway." He mimed pumping a handle. "Just keep paddling and don't let 'em drop, Walt, and you'll eventually get there."

"Thanks—your confidence is contagious." I turned, and the Ferg met me as I got to the ladder leading up into the cockpit. He swallowed and nodded his head up and down like a nervous horse. "Are you sure you don't want me to go?"

I acted like I was actually thinking about it. "Yep, why don't you go and I'll stay here?" He looked as if the muscles in his heart had frozen. "I'm just kidding; this is my harebrained idea and if the previous sheriff of Absaroka County and the present sheriff of Absaroka County get killed, the citizens are going to need a new one."

He laughed. "Maybe, but I don't want the job under those conditions, so you two be careful, okay?"

The man didn't seem to hold it against me that I'd passed over him to the position I now held. "You'd be a good one, Ferg."

A cantankerous voice bellowed from the echoing insides of the big Mitchell. "Anytime you and Betty Grable are through kissing and saying good-bye, I've got a plane to fly to Denver, damnit."

7

"Open cowl flaps, Toots."

Julie's hand moved steadily as it pulled a lever on her left, but I was not reassured to see that the flight manual for the Mitchell VB-25J was open in her lap. "Mixture control in full rich position."

The old Doolittle Raider pushed another set of levers forward in turn. "Throttle position one thousand rpm—battery disconnect switches on."

Standing up, I peered through the windshield at the men waiting to open the doors and then close them after we taxied out. Rick was positioned in front with a fire extinguisher, which was not a comforting sight.

Lucian's fingers snapped across the instrument panel. "Switching on ignition and fuel booster pumps." He glanced back at me. "Nervous, Troop?"

I looked around, looking for seatbelts—I was on the jump seat behind Lucian and finally found a harness, draped it over my shoulders, and buckled in. "Not if you're not."

"Oh, hell, we got a one-legged pilot who hasn't flown one of these things in about a hundred years." He grinned at Julie, her bright yellow ball cap embroidered with a small bear bearing the words PIPER CUB, her green headphones pushed up and parked at a jaunty angle over one ear. "A copilot that in flight-time reality has barely even sat in one." He glanced around the cockpit. "A hangar queen that's ready for the salvage yard, and a snowstorm that's going to try and blow us into the ground near Wichita . . . What could go wrong?" He glanced at his lovely copilot. "Energizing right starter and priming."

She took a swig from the plastic jug and then lodged it between her seat and the fuselage. "Roger that."

"Mesh the starter, Toots."

Her smile faded, for a number of reasons. "Me?"

He half grinned a roguish grin. "You gotta start sometime, Angel." He turned back to the controls. "Just don't hold 'em on too long or you'll burn out our booster coils." He turned to the right, and we watched as one of the 1,700-horsepower engines sputtered, kicked, seemed to rhythmically explode, and then began chopping the air in the hangar with its three-blade propeller. Lucian hollered to be heard above the racket, "Left engine starter energized and primed!"

Julie yelled back, "Left engine starter meshed!"

I'd thought I was going to be deafened by the sound of one of the supercharged Wright Cyclone engines, but when the other coughed to life I was sure of it. The roar of the things was tremendous, and the heaving of the plane's airframe as Lucian tapped the oil pressure gauges and they settled at forty pounds of pressure was thunderous. "Lady and gentleman, the Mitchell B-25 medium bomber—the fastest way in the world to turn a hundred-and-thirty-octane aviation fuel into pure noise!"

I watched the rotation of the propellers as they caught up with themselves, almost as if they'd slowed, and then as they accelerated, disappeared into a whirl of pitched power, the yellow tips of the blades creating a wreath of deadly, cautionary color in line with the red stripes on the fuselage.

Lucian yelled again. "Weapons!"

Julie stared at the instruments for a moment and then quizzically at him.

He laughed, and I could still smell the bourbon in his breath. "Just seeing if you were paying attention!"

White exhaust smoke filtered through the cockpit from the numerous holes and cracks in the fuselage, stinging my eyes and making it hard to see—effectively, I was now blind, along with being deaf. "What's all that smoke—are we on fire?"

"It's caused by the oil left over in the cylinders—same stuff that waterproofed your boots. It'll clear once I throttle up." I felt a clawlike grip grab my hand and place it on a handle at the center between the two seats, and the brim of Lucian's hat poked the side of my face. "Stop worrying, Marine. You just keep a hand on that lever!" He pounded a forefinger against a small black dial on the control panel. "Julie says the main engine pumps are weak on this ship. Don't you let that hydraulic pressure drop below where I've made that mark, you understand?"

I leaned forward, searching for the mark and the designated instrument with my eyes burning. "What happens if I do?"

"We lose brakes and can't operate the landing gear or

flaps and crash, you damn fool!" He swiveled in the aluminum seat with its minimal padding, slid back the glass to the outside, yanked off his hat, and waved the silver belly back and forth to indicate to Rick we were ready to taxi and to let us pass before we all died of asphyxiation. "Stand away and let this Baker-Two-Bits bitch fly!"

Rick stepped back, the doors opened, and the snowstorm charged inside to get us, blankets of white flapping like covers on the hangar floor, blistering out of the night like hordes of tiny albino hornets.

Lucian pushed the throttle forward, and the big plane lurched ahead with its nose dipping before rising steadily as we really began moving. I know it was only my imagination, but it was as if I could hear the snow complain as the big tires rolled over it, the B-25 angling to the right as we moved out of that hangar like a rocket ship, like a steam train, like a horse galloping home.

There would be people who would argue with me, but I swear that old bird pranced out of that building and into the snow like a beer-commercial Clydesdale, a mobile fortress shooting into the black and white of the night before Christmas with the two spinning propellers pulling us inexorably forward like corkscrewed fate.

When I looked up at Lucian, he grinned with an absolute conviction and fanned the side of the plane with his cowboy hat like a saddle-bronc rider yelling as loud as he could to be heard above the din. "Powder River, let 'er buck!"

Slim Pickens as pilot.

We were doomed.

8

The hydraulic pressure had already started to drop slightly as we taxied but rose as I pumped the lever.

While jacking the red handle, I noticed that some wise-acre had hung an old keychain of the state emblem off of the yellow escape hatch canopy frame above our heads. The unnamed wag had attached a small, gold-colored bucking horse, complete with hatless rider fanning the brass chain from which the lucky trinket swung, along with a few beads and a tin-cone bell from a Cheyenne Fancy Dress dance costume.

Maybe it had been some pilot over Normandy, maybe some firefighter, but it was likely that he, like me, was looking for a charm or a totem—some sort of medicine that would keep him alive. You'd be amazed at the things you'll do when you think the next few moments might be your last—even the smallest of signs can loom large like irrevocable messages from the ether.

In Vietnam and even now, I kept a beaded medicine bag that Henry had given me years earlier, trusting the Bear's intuition and spirituality. Unconsciously, my hand crept up and delved into the inside pocket of my sheepskin coat, and I ran my thumb over the hard glass beads strung along the elk hide for luck, a habit I'd picked up during the Tet Offensive. I could feel the different items I'd placed inside, things that I treasured and that only I knew about.

There were ghosts out there in that whistling snow and blow, ancient voices that could rise in harmony for or against you—and I was bound that they would be for the girl named after the sun goddess Amaterasu, who shone over heaven. It was strange, but the rhythm of the engines began sounding like drums, and it was almost as if they were establishing a driving force to combat the wind.

Glancing around the cockpit, I wondered at the turn of the fates that would put a hurt Japanese child in such a beast like *Steamboat*—the same kind of plane that Lucian had flown thirty seconds over Tokyo to drop bombs on her ancestors, but this time on a suicide mission to carry a wounded Japanese child to Denver on a hellacious, storm-filled night.

As Lucian closed the window, put on his snow-patched Stetson, and continued giving the bomber more throttle, I amused myself by thinking about the real Steamboat, the horse that had become the longest-running license plate motif in the world.

Steamboat didn't start there or on the patches of the Wyoming National Guardsmen who served in the 148th Field Artillery Regiment in World War I, but rather as a colt foaled on the Frank Foss Ranch near Chugwater, Wyoming, the progeny of a massive Percheron stallion and a hot-blooded Mexican mare. A product of his breeding, he grew strong, so strong in fact that when castrated, he slammed his head against the ground so hard that he broke cartilage loose in his long nose, resulting in a distinctive whistling sound when he breathed—hence the name, Steamboat.

For many a rodeo cowboy, it was the last thing they heard before hitting the ground.

Solid black with three white stockings, the horse enjoyed parades and Wild West shows, where he was known to keep time to the music the bands played; but, docile while being handled, there was something he could not abide—riders. The bucker would not allow a man to stay on top of him, and, rapidly becoming the toast of stock providers, he performed in every major rodeo in the United States for years.

There is a great deal of controversy as to who the rider is on the license plate, from Jake Maring and Guy Holt to Stub Farlow, but there is no controversy as to the fact that none of them ever rode the horse known as the Lord of the Plains or the King of the Hurricane Deck to a standstill. Allen True captured the spirit of the animal for the princely sum of seventy-five dollars when Secretary of State Lester C. Hunt commissioned him to depict the horse and rider as the design for the 1936 Wyoming license plate.

Steamboat's story didn't end well, though—the legendary horse fell victim to blood poisoning due to an altercation with a barbed-wire fence while penned during a lightning storm in Salt Lake City. He was returned to Wyoming where veterinarians made the critical judgment that there was no way to save the swollen, dying horse, and a rifle was fetched to dispatch the animal and end its suffering—the gun, coincidently, having been owned by another famous Wyoming legend, Tom Horn.

On a cold, gray October 14 in 1914, the blast of that rifle

ended the career of one of the greatest bucking horses of all time. Legend promotes the story that Steamboat was buried under the hard-packed earth of Frontier Park in Cheyenne, a place where uncounted cowboys and mighty buckers have gone seat to saddle, but the legend belies the truth. I'd spoken with one of the men who was there. Standing under the old wooden bleachers with Paul R. Hanson, he told me, "People say that he was buried at Frontier Park, but that's not true." The old cowpuncher looked off to the distance, looking for something, maybe some way to bring things back and change them. "He was buried at the old city dump where he was destroyed. A desecration, Walter, and that's for sure."

The bucking horse charm shot forward and swung back and forth as the big aircraft lurched to a stop, the wheels sliding on the snow as Dickens's words hung in my mind, in my mouth, and on the end of that chain: "Much they saw, and far they went, and many homes they visited, but always with a happy end. The Spirit stood beside sick beds, and they were cheerful; on foreign lands, and they were close at home; by struggling men, and they were patient in their greater hope. . . ."

9

"The wind is blowing so hard the snow isn't even sticking to the airplane." Julie's voice broke in on my thoughts as she and Lucian strained forward, trying to see what it was that had materialized between the bright-white runway lights. "What the heck is that?"

Lucian shook his head as he fumbled with his headset in order to pull the ear cups over his ears, no mean feat while wearing a cowboy hat. He adjusted the microphone. "Hey . . ." He paused, leaned toward his copilot with a fist around the mic, and whispered to Julie, "What the hell is our call sign again?"

She grimaced and looked down at the flight plan and the assortment of papers in her lap. "Raider N4030 and the personal designation LC that you added to the end when we filed our flight plan."

I glanced around and spotted another pair of headphones on a coiled cord—I'm smart that way—so I snatched them off and put them over my ears in the same fashion as my old boss, which not only enabled me to hear the conversation but muffled some of the engine noise.

Before Lucian could transmit the question, Rick, whose voice sounded tinny and far away even though he was just a little ways behind us, started speaking. Static. "Raider November 4030 Lima Charlie this is Durant UNICOM. I have your clearance from Salt Lake as follows—ATC—clears LIFE-GUARD NOVEMBER 4030 LIMA CHARLIE to Denver Stapleton Airport VIA THE CRAZYWOMAN THREE ONE NINE RADIAL, CRAZYWOMAN VOR, AS FILED, MAINTAIN ONE THREE THOUSAND, CONTACT SALT LAKE CITY CENTER FREQUENCY ONE TWO SEVEN POINT SEVEN FIVE, SQUAWK FOUR ONE TWO SEVEN, CLEARANCE VOID IF NOT OFF BY ZERO FOUR THREE ZERO."

As Julie copied the clearance, I watched Lucian's lips move and then opt for words I'd heard them say numerous times before. "Jesus H. Christ, Durant UNICOM, who the hell parked an iceberg out here on our runway?"

I rose up and looked over both their heads at the front of the plane where a pile of snow the size of an eighteen-wheeler created a hill stretching the entire width of the runway. "You've got to be kidding."

Rick's voice was weary. Static. "Is it out near the wind sock to the north?"

Julie sat up and looked through her side window and turned back. "Roger that."

Static. "Must be where those idiots sometimes dump the snow. I guess with the wind coming in from the northwest, the damn thing acted like a snow fence and filled up the runway." He sighed, his voice indicating utter defeat. "You guys might as well come on back . . ."

There was silence on the airwaves as Lucian, looking out the side window into the darkness, broken only by the horizontal lines of snow, casually held a hand out to his copilot. "Hey, you got another stick of that Beemans?"

She glanced back at me and then fumbled the pack from her pocket and handed him a piece.

Slowly, the old Raider unwrapped the gum and popped it in his mouth, and, tossing the wrapper over his right shoulder like a pinch of salt, he pulled the mic in close. "Hey, Rick, what's the distance between this wind sock and the terminal?"

Static. "Only about three hundred yards, so don't you even think about it."

I watched as he chewed his gum and then punched one of the levers forward, causing the big bird to pivot on one tire so that she turned around and faced the vague and furry lights of the Durant terminal building like a picador in a bull-ring. His head rose slowly as he looked from under the cowboy hat and down the blue-lit taxiway, his jaw set. "Hell, we woulda had a crosswind on the main runway anyway; this puts us directly into a forty-five-knot headwind. With the limited fuel quantity we're carrying, *Steamboat*'s light enough to make it." He inclined his head toward his copilot. "Full brakes, Angel."

Dumbfounded, she swung her head around to look at him.

Lucian roared. "Help me hold 'em, damn it, full brakes!" Julie did as she'd been ordered, and then he turned and looked back at me. "And why aren't you pumping that handle? My hydraulic pressure is dropping!"

I began pumping like a madman. "Lucian, what are you planning on doing?"

The black brows crowded over those mahogany eyes and studied the darkness ahead and found it wanting, his voice low. "You don't have to yell, I can hear you through the microphone—it's voice-activated."

"What are you doing?" This time I whispered.

Static. "Raider LC, there's no way that heap will clear the terminal building."

I watched as he reached up and pulled the headset cord from the panel, letting it fall into his lap, Rick's voice still pleading in my earphones. Static. "Lucian, you're going to kill them all. There's no way in these conditions that you're going to get the altitude you need to make it over this building. Hell, you're going to kill us, too!"

The hand with a grip I'd seen crack walnuts reached down and slowly ran up the throttles on both engines, the force of them shifting the weight of the entire aircraft forward. The pitch seemed ready to throw the pistons through the supercharged cylinder heads when Lucian leaned in center and yelled in Julie's face, "When I release these throttles with my right hand, you grab them and hold them all the way forward while I grab the yoke and take us up. We're going to need every bridled horse this old nag's got—you read me?"

She nodded and then turned to look at my widened eyes with hers.

Lucian gestured toward his missing left leg. "Run the pedals and hold some right rudder pressure to counter the left torque of the propellers; I'll do the flying, you just keep it pointed down the runway!" He nodded, as if remembering something else. "If we lose an engine, shut the other one down—at least that way we crash straight." He laughed. "It's been known to happen with this cayuse!"

I tried reason one more time, reaching up and tapping his leather-clad arm. "Lucian?"

He ignored me and, pulling his hat down tighter, cracked his gum and gestured toward the control. "Release brakes!"

Julie turned, looked at him for a split moment, and did as she was told; *Steamboat* jumped forward kicking slightly sideways as if the chute gate at a rodeo had just been opened. Lucian compensated by leading with the left throttle to equalize any unbalanced propeller thrust before turning them over to Julie as we rushed forward. His hand gently pulled left on the yoke as the gusts grew stronger, and I watched as his shoulders gathered with the exertion.

I rose up a little in my seat and could see the lights of the terminal growing rapidly closer, Rick's voice still coming through my headset. Static. "Raider Lima Charlie, you need to shut the engines down on that thing right now!"

The brim of his cowboy hat diverted to Julie for only a second, and he winked as he released the throttles and moved his hand away as his copilot strained with both of hers to push the levers forward. Gripping the wheel of the medium bomber, Lucian compensated even further, turning left.

I couldn't help but drop the mic from my mouth and yell, "Is it the wind?"

His right cheek bunched in a smile as he growled, "What wind?"

I shook my head, but my attention was drawn to the windshield and the looming vision of the concrete-block building that was bearing down on us—it looked to me as if we were going to barrel right into it. I glanced at Julie, figuring her experience in these types of things was far superior to mine, but her reaction did not inspire confidence.

Our copilot was still pressing the throttles forward, but her body was involuntarily leaning back in an attempt to avoid the oncoming crash.

Rick's voice continued to plead in my ears. Static. "Lucian!"

I looked up again, and I could see the old Doolittle Raider's lips moving as he counted off the snow-covered yards. He had been a pain in my ass at almost every turn since he'd hired me as a deputy, but things had escalated when he'd halfheartedly run against me, doing almost anything he could to sabotage his own campaign—looking distracted and disinterested during the debates, going out of his way to insult the different social organizations, and even publicly supporting me in an interview in the *Durant Courant*.

Static. "Raider LC, you need to abort!"

I'd won in a landslide, and when Lucian decided to leave his ancestral ranch house and more than ten thousand acres to take up residency at the Durant Home for Assisted Living, I had felt sorry for him. With his influence dead and his poker friends dying, I proposed the idea that I play chess with him on Tuesday nights at the home, but with the responsibilities of the new job, a marriage, and a child, I hadn't played a single game with him yet.

He had been drinking more and still played poker occasionally—there was even talk of a tryst with a woman on Thursday afternoons at the Euskadi Hotel, where I had abducted him from the bar what already seemed like a hundred years ago.

Static. "Lucian!"

Even before his retirement, he had obtained the reputation of something past its time—something dangerous, like a gunfighter that Absaroka County and Durant had needed but, now that all the bad guys were gone, didn't anymore. Displaced and discarded.

But there he sat with all the muscle his three limbs could muster, flying an ancient airplane into the storm of the century for the sake of a small wounded girl.

"We're not going to make it." Julie's voice was high and strained through the earphones, but I could hear it as if it were my own thoughts.

Through the windshield, the blurred image of the terminal building's two stories topped with a tiny observation tower and its surrounding chain-link fence flew toward us in what seemed to be a bizarre game of chicken with the big Mitchell.

"We only had four hundred and sixty-seven feet on the Hornet when we flew the raid!" Lucian was yelling over the noise now, but his voice was strong and steady.

I noticed that Julie had pulled back off the throttles as her sense of self-preservation caused her to lean even farther back from the impending crash, so I reached up, placed my hand over hers, and forced the levers to full as the Cyclone engine superchargers screamed. I felt a slight bump as the nose of the B-25 lifted and watched as Lucian released some of the pressure on the yoke but then abruptly yanked to the left with a sudden gust and then slowly pulled back, like Atlas, lifting the world.

"Hell, I took one off in less than three hundred feet in training!"

I could feel the friction of the tires leaving the snow and the sudden rush of flight, but the second story of the terminal and, more important, the tiny observation shack that sat on top still towered over us.

Lucian pulled the yoke back even more and with the next blast from the arctic front veered *Steamboat* into a turn that must've clipped something on the right wingtip. The Mitchell shuddered for only a second and then flew over the parking lot, where under the illuminated globes of the dusk-to-dawn lights I could see everyone standing on the tarmac; I guess they all had evacuated the terminal.

I didn't blame them one damn bit.

The crazy bastard even laughed. "Room to spare!" The big bird righted as Lucian instructed Julie to apply pressure to the left rudder control to compensate for his missing leg as another gust hammered the back of the bomber in an attempt to send us over the edge of the plateau into the city dump.

"Gotta get this dirty bird cleaned up." Lucian strained as he commanded Julie to raise the landing gear and looked back at me. "Are you pumping that handle?"

I yanked my hand off the throttle as Julie raised the gear and replaced me. I began jacking the lever for all it was worth as the old sheriff steered us in a tight turn, away from the glow of the small valley where the streetlights shone a ribbon of diffused gold against the foothills of the Bighorn Mountains. I could feel the first flip of my stomach as the B-25 shuddered with the winds coming over those mountains like long, icy tendrils grabbing for our controls.

We dropped a bit as we came off the plateau above town, and Julie raised the flaps. We blew over the well-lit haze of Main Street only feet above the three-story buildings, and dragged a vortex of powdery snow down the main drag like a tidal wave, rattling the windows of the Euskadi Bar.

I rose up as high as my harness would allow and looked through the side window as *Steamboat* banked and climbed over the plateau above Durant, the thundering, radial engines hammering the cold air like drumming hooves. The ghostly horse bucked, weaved, and then righted itself over the junkyard, its cars, abandoned refrigerators, and washers and dryers cluttering the snowy hillside to the east of town.

As we accelerated and climbed into the clouds, I could vaguely make out Rick's send-off in my headphones—evidently he was the only one who hadn't joined the others in the parking lot and given up the ship. Static. "Godspeed, Raider Lima Charlie."

Glancing up at the gold bucking horse, with his beads and bell still hanging from the yellow frame of the escape hatch, I watched as they clattered together knowing they were making a sound but so small it would never be heard above the racket of the engines. Reaching up, I steadied the swinging charm and thought about the dump where the great horse had been finally and ignobly laid to rest—and was just glad we hadn't followed him.

Static. "And Godspeed, *Steamboat*."

10

We were still climbing, and I watched my breath fog my words. "Is there really heat in this thing?"

"Some." Lucian, having reattached his headphones, laughed. "There must be some of those bird's nests still in the intake of the cabin heater. Good thing the carburetor heat is working, though, 'cause we might be running into some ice south of here. So far it's too cold to stick."

I'd been able to button my coat over my coveralls with my free hand, but my arm was aching from pumping the damned red handle. "How long is it going to take to get to Stapleton?"

The old Raider stared at the instruments and reached up to tap the gauge. He paused for a moment and then fumbled his bifocals from the pocket of the coveralls that he wore underneath the leather jacket he must've acquired from his locker. He slipped on the prescription glasses and tapped the small, black gauge again, as if getting its attention.

Lucian gradually started to level off *Steamboat*. "We're

almost to thirteen thousand feet; I'd be truly amazed if this Dodo bird got up to two hundred fifty miles an hour true airspeed, even with the tailwind we got runnin' up our ass. I'm bettin' we're gonna get maybe two hundred thirty-six knots out of her."

I looked at the gauge and rubbed my sore arm. "So, it's not doing two fifty?" The distance on the wall planning chart next to Rick's office showed 285 miles to Denver; at 250 it would only take us barely over an hour.

Lucian cast a black, glimmering eye back at me and then, tossing a thumb my way, grinned at Julie. "Marine."

Pulling a whiz wheel out of her backpack and running the numbers, Julie smiled, pitying the poor ground troop. "Two hundred eighty-five *nautical* miles, Walt; the distance is actually three hundred twenty-eight statute miles to Denver. The conversion is one point fifteen mph to a knot, and according to Lucian's estimate we're doing two hundred thirty-six nautical miles an hour." She glanced at the old, bold pilot, then at her whiz wheel. "Um . . . two hundred and seventy mph?"

He nodded. "Two hundred and seventy-two, Toots."

I interrupted the love fest. "So, how long to Denver?"

Turning back to the instrument panel, he surveyed his domain. "Why, your arm getting tired?"

"Yep."

"You can stop."

I continued pumping. "I don't want to crash."

"Well, you can stop; we're good on hydraulic pressure with the gear and flaps up till we have to land. You're going to feel like you flew down there flappin' one arm if you have to do that the whole way." I felt the rattletrap settle and the nose drop as he eased off the throttle and trimmed the aircraft in a heading due south. "I'm leveling us off at thirteen thousand and setting the engines into an economic cruising speed . . ."

I held up my other hand. "Wait. Did you just say thirteen thousand feet?"

"I did." He smiled. "It's the only way we can fly direct and clear Laramie Peak. Why, you got a problem with that?"

The radio headset crackled to life in all our heads.

Static. "NOVEMBER 4030 Lima Charlie—Salt Lake City Center—say your position and confirm your destination."

Lucian keyed his mic. "Roger Salt Lake—Raider NOVEMBER 4030 Lima Charlie—we are a LIFEGUARD flight southbound from Durant, Wyoming, at thirteen thousand, on the CRAZY WOMAN three-one-nine radial, five north enroute Stapleton."

Static. "Raider 4030 Lima Charlie—Salt Lake—no radar contact, recycle transponder."

The old sheriff laughed a knowing look at his copilot. "Salt Lake—LIFEGUARD Raider Lima Charlie—unless you've got radar that can pick me up without a transponder, you aren't going to pick me up at all."

There was a long pause.

Static. "Raider Lima Charlie, are you saying that you are not transponder equipped?"

"Roger that, Salt Lake."

"Raider Lima Charlie—Salt Lake—say your estimate for Stapleton airport."

He slipped what looked like an old pocket watch from the hand warmer of the A2 flight jacket and keyed his mic again. "Son, I really don't have any choice but to do it the old-fashioned way. This plane I'm flying has me and an old Elgin Type A8 stopwatch; trust me, that'll get the job done. Estimating Stapleton at time 0630 ZULU and don't forget, we are LIFEGUARD and request priority handling."

There was an even longer pause.

Static. "Raider Lima Charlie—Salt Lake—we don't seem to have you registered in any of our books, confirm you are a vintage aircraft?"

The old sheriff smiled. "Salt Lake—Raider Lima Charlie— we are flying *Steamboat*, a magnificently restored Mitchell, VB-25J medium bomber, actually the VIP aircraft used by Dwight D. Eisenhower during the Normandy invasion, brilliant, polished aluminum in color."

I glanced around at the cracked and glazed windows, candy wrappers, cigarette butts, and general detritus on the floor, along with the gaps in the fuselage that felt as if they were channeling the freezing wind in and through us, and tried not to laugh out loud.

Lucian cupped a hand over his mic and winked at Julie and me. "What they don't know won't hurt 'em."

The disembodied voice crackled through our headsets again. Static. "And this is a medical emergency flight?"

The old sheriff took his hand away. "Roger that, Salt Lake."

Static. "Well, you're Denver Center's problem here in about three minutes, not that they'll know it if you're without radar contact or flying in the treetops . . ."

Lucian keyed the mic and glanced at Julie in apology for the old joke. "Son, haven't you heard about Wyoming? Why, there's a good-looking woman behind every tree . . . There just aren't any trees."

Static. "Raider Lima Charlie, we've got reports of heavy weather in your vicinity—can you confirm?"

Turbulence rocked the plane like a washing machine again,

and Lucian swore but then calmed his on-air voice with a bit of sarcasm. "Salt Lake—clear as a bell where we are right now."

Static. "Raider Lima Charlie—Salt Lake—will advise Denver Center of your status, Contact Denver Center on ONE THREE FIVE DECIMAL SIX."

"Roger that, signing off." Our pilot turned and addressed the crew. "Not much of a sense of humor, huh?"

"Me, either, at the moment." I rested my hand but left it on the lever, just in case he changed his mind. "So, how long is it going to take?"

"'Bout an hour and twenty minutes. Hell, we're liable to be there before midnight if our luck holds." He brought up his wristwatch and studied it. "Merry Christmas."

I unbuckled my harness and stood up, expecting to see the rolling, snow-covered hills of northern Wyoming. "I can't see a thing—it's pitch black out there. You sure you know where we are?"

"Relatively speaking, right now according to our only VOR navigation radio, we are almost between Powder Junction to the west and the Pumpkin Buttes to the east, but the reception is very weak, and I wouldn't bet on how long it holds out."

"I feel so much better."

He gestured toward the lever. "I'll let you know when you need to get your exercise again." I eased back into the tiny seat, flexed my bicep, and slipped on my gloves as he continued talking over his shoulder. "Not to make you feel worse, but we're picking up some ice." He pulled an old military flashlight from a holder, hit the switch, and then banged it on the instrument panel until it gave out with a yellowish beam. He shone it onto the left engine. "That motor is running rough—the carburetor heat must not be fully working on number one. Because we're not pressurized, we can't climb out of it—we have no crew oxygen. Our course puts Laramie Peak below us somewhere right off our nose, so if the icing gets worse we're going to have to change to the east and descend." He glanced through the windshield into the rapidly passing night. "That'll cost us time and fuel."

I smoothed my mustache and could feel some ice building up on it. Suddenly I heard a loud bang, followed by several more—something was hitting the side of *Steamboat*'s fuselage. "What the hell is that?"

"Ice slinging off the props." He sat up a little more and looked through the windshield with his flashlight again. "In daylight we could follow I-25 as long as it stayed black, but that's academic since it's night, and with them closing the roads it'll start piling up with snow or the scud would shut us out, and we'd still have to rely on radio navigation, and without the old iron compass and my A8, we'd be FUBAR. You know what that means, right?"

"Yep. Wait, what's the iron compass?"

Lucian growled. "Railroad tracks."

"And scud is ground fog." Julie took another swig from her jug and swallowed loudly. "At night you would need landing lights to see the road, but B-25s didn't come equipped."

The Raider smiled and reached underneath the main panel to flip what appeared to be a hidden switch. "Yeah, well, Angel, this one does."

Both Julie and I looked out the windows and could see nothing but a solid white snowscape of flakes shooting past, undulating and illuminated by the lights that glowed from each wing, thrilling but disorienting enough to cause my stomach to try and crawl up my throat.

"But you never turn on landing lights at night in a heavy snowstorm or scud if you want to see anything—everyone knows that, too, right, Toots?"

The blonde, ignoring the sarcasm, looked at Lucian. "How did you know about those?"

Turning off the lights, he settled back in his seat and adjusted the left throttle. "What, you think this is the first time *Steamboat* and I ever danced the hurricane deck?"

"Not now, I don't."

He peered at the stopwatch and rose up a little as if to look over the nose of the craft into the blackness. "Powder Junction; we're making good time."

He sat back down and glanced at his copilot. "You got 'er, Toots?"

She made a face and then nodded as he turned back to look at me. "You ever hear of Operation Haylift?"

I nodded. "Rings a bell."

"Before your time, really." He shot a look at Julie again. "Both of you." He noticed something on the dash and absently reached up to tap one of the instruments. "Back in '49 we had one of the worst winters we'd ever had since 1889, which, I would like to add, was before my time. The one in '49 was dubbed the Winter of the Great White Ruin; millions of sheep and cattle were stranded in snowdrifts without feed, sometimes caught with herders with their horses and mules, entire ranches snowed in. Well, I got a call from Greybull and he wants to know if I can take off and land a B-25 in short distance, and I tell him, hell, if you've got an aircraft carrier I can take her off that." He adjusted his hat and flipped up the collar on his leather jacket, the cold evidently getting to him, too. "Mostly they used C82s, called 'em Flying Boxcars for Operation Haylift, but we used anything that was around . . . We dropped 525 tons of alfalfa in the first week, fed a million sheep and a hundred thousand head of cattle, not to mention all the sheepherders and ranchers we saved." He smiled. "Wasn't all roses, though. We had one ol' fella—we dropped the first big, heavy bale and it took out his front porch; then we dropped another on his corral and collapsed half of it; then we finished the job by dropping one on his wash house, which had his wife's brand-new wringer-washer in it. He got on his horse and was able to get to a neighbor's place, which had a phone, and called us up: Please don't drop any more hay on my place, or my wife's gonna divorce me . . ." Lucian reached out and patted the throttles of the big plane. "The reason I'm telling you this story—this was the plane I flew back in '49."

He glanced around the cockpit. "You'd be amazed how connected to these things you can get." He tipped his silver belly hat back and indicated to Julie that he could take the yoke now and fly the aircraft as he turned forward but talked over his shoulder at me. "Does the doc know how to use these headphones?"

I thought about how silent it had been from the rear of the Mitchell. "He mentioned them when I was talking to him before we took off. You think they're busted or he doesn't know how to turn them on?"

He shrugged. "It's quiet."

I nodded and finished the hackneyed cinematic statement for him, ". . . it's too quiet."

Shifting in the seat and peering through the dim glow of instrumentation in the rear of the cockpit, I spotted the crawl-space above the bomb bay. "Through there?"

"Yes—unless you wanna climb out the window here and crawl around."

I glanced at Julie. "She's small; how come she can't do it?"

"'Cause I'm gonna need her help to determine the maximum range that can be squeezed out of every drop of gasoline by setting the correct throttle, prop pitch, and mixing controls—and by the way, she's helping me fly the damn plane." He pulled back and then pushed forward, and I could feel my stomach once again attempting to leave my body through my mouth. I grabbed the seat underneath me. "I knew that ridge was around here somewhere." After making sure Julie had the con again, he pulled out a small notepad along with a stubby golf pencil that had also been hiding in his pocket. "First thing I ever taught you was that a short pencil's better than a long memory, Troop." He licked the point and shot me another look. "What, you wanna crash?"

"No, I thought I was pretty clear about that." A thought became even clearer as I freed myself from my abbreviated bench seat and leaned forward. "Hey, we've got enough fuel to make it to Denver, right?" He busied himself, running the numbers on the pad and looking at his wristwatch and the vintage stopwatch—the year of our Lord nineteen hundred and eighty-eight, and we were down to this.

He tapped the gauge again. "Well, one of three things . . ."

I stopped moving. "Oh, why do I not like the sound of that?"

"Either that knucklehead Rick shorted us on fuel, our indicators are off . . ." He stared at the gauges, giving all of them a tap for history's sake or maybe that's what pilots did, tap gauges. "Or . . ."

"Or what?"

"We've got ourselves a leak."

"How bad?" I took a strange comfort in the tone of Julie's voice, sounding as concerned as mine.

"She'll hold 974 gallons, but that ain't what we've got."

My turn to swallow. "How much do we have?"

"About a quarter of that." The old Raider scrubbed the stubble on his face with a knotty hand and then leaned back in his seat with his lips moving as they had when he'd been counting the yards when it seemed we were hell-bent on crashing into the terminal building. His hand dropped, and he made a few more calculations; then he nodded, speaking mostly to himself but perhaps a little to *Steamboat*. "At this rate, we'll make it, though—just."

Stooping in the cockpit, I stepped around my seat—these things weren't made for anybody six foot five. "I can't tell you how reassured I am." They ignored me as I hung my headset on the back of my seat. Lucian began going over the figures with Julie and making adjustments to the intimidating number of switches, knobs, and levers on the ancient plane. "If either of you gets bored, feel free to take a turn on the lever there."

11

There was a small space at the rear of the cockpit that looked as if it was for the radio and possibly the bombardier, but what did I know? The plane rocked and dropped as I grabbed the rails in a weightless state, looking back to see the two pilots attempting to right the aircraft; evidently, the real teeth of the storm were catching up with us.

I placed a foot on the small ladder, which was bolted to the rear bulkhead that led to the dark crawlspace above the bomb bay. I took a few steps up and forced my bulk into the aluminum sheathing, aware that the empty space and a few doors that had their own ideas about staying closed were the only thing between me and a doozy of a couple thousand foot drop. There were handles on the side to assist, so I pulled myself along, feeling like I was working in a coal mine.

There was light at the other end of the crawlspace, and I have to admit that I was relieved to get to the other side; I raised my head to look into the dimly lit amidships and the rear of the B-25.

The gurney was still attached the way it had been, the IVs, oxygen tanks, battery packs, and assorted medical equipment not having moved, but the other two passengers were not in their seats. The child's grandmother was on the floor beside the covered, ventilated gurney, but I couldn't see Isaac anywhere.

Mrs. Oda looked up, very happy to see me, and yelled above the constant drone of the engines, *"Yokatta!"*

I maneuvered a turnaround and clambered down the ladder with all the grace of a wounded buffalo; I still couldn't locate the doc. *Steamboat* bucked again, and I grabbed hold of the inside fuselage to steady myself before venturing farther, sure that if I didn't, I would likely land on someone.

Feeling a knot in my stomach, I kneeled by the woman, pulled back the blankets beside her, and discovered Isaac, out cold, with a good-sized goose egg on his forehead. "The plane knocked him out?"

"Hai." I noticed the fine quality of her features and the absolute white of her hair; if I'd been casting a Japanese empress, I don't think I could've found anyone that looked more the role than Mrs. Oda.

"How long has he been unconscious? Did it happen when we took off?"

She nodded twice, but I was pretty sure she didn't understand a word I was saying.

I figured Isaac must've fallen on takeoff before he could get in his seat and get his harness on. I checked his pulse, which appeared to be fine, and then gave him a few gentle smacks on the face. "Doc, hey, Doc!"

His eyelids compressed and then opened, his eyes focused through the thick lenses of his glasses, and he turned to me. "Walter?"

"None other."

Listening to the engines, he raised his voice. "Where are we?"

"Considering the alternative, the good news is—still aloft."

A bit confused but rapidly gathering his wits, he looked up at the woman. "Oh my God, how is the girl?"

I peeled the blankets away, save one, figuring he was going to need it, and helped him to his feet as he massaged the side of his head. "You're going to have to tell us."

I moved Mrs. Oda onto her seat and buckled her in, but just as I turned, the plane veered again, this time banking, sending Isaac and me into the side of the fuselage and one of the Plexiglas windows; we both looked out into the darkness and then slid onto the steel grating of the floor. Luckily, the doc landed on top of me, and we lay there for a moment before *Steamboat* settled back into a level position.

Isaac looked around. "Has the entire flight been like this?"

Half picking him up, I sat him against the bulkhead. "It hasn't been that bad until now. We're headed due south, but the storm front is coming in southeast, so we're just on the edge, but I think it's catching up."

Isaac struggled to a standing position, holding on to the ladder. "Can't we go any faster?"

"No. We're stuck, and whatever happens, we've just got to ride it out."

He nodded and approached the gurney to check the IVs and battery pack on the ventilator attached to the girl. He disconnected one of the bottles and hooked up another, all the time trying to explain over the constant drone of the radial engines. "The fluids must run the whole time; this is the most important part of burn resuscitation."

Steamboat rocked again but not quite so violently, and the doc pulled his stethoscope from under his coveralls and jacket, fumbling the stems into his ears, sneaking his hand under the plastic tent, and placing it over Amaterasu's heart. I studied his face and then watched as he moved the device on her chest.

He glanced at me with a hard look. "I'm going to need your help." His tone froze me for a second, and I watched as he fished a blood pressure cuff from one of his medical supply bags attached to the gurney. He spoke through the side of his mouth directly into my ear as he glanced at the tense older woman harnessed into her seat. "I can't hear her heart."

My eyes bugged. "What?"

He shook his head and gestured toward the interior of the cabin. "With all the racket, I can't hear her heart—at least, I hope it's because of all the engine noise."

"What can I do?"

He unrolled the cuff and began attaching it to the child's limp arm. "Hang on to me and don't let me fly all over the inside of this damnable contraption while I'm working, for a start."

I reached over and gripped the inside brace of the fuselage and then grabbed a fistful of Isaac's baggy coveralls at the small of his back. I watched as he uncovered Amaterasu— Mrs. Oda inched a little forward in her seat so that she could also see.

Only half the girl's face was visible under the bandages, but even with the swelling and the soot burns around her nostrils where the plastic tubing entered her body, you could see the resemblance to her grandmother. Very pale, she was maybe ten or eleven, very close to Cady's age.

"The residual burns on her face were caused by the hot steam that burns the mucosa . . ." The doc's hands were deft and professional as he pumped up the cuff and deflated it slowly while holding on to the girl's wrist to check the radial artery. He repeated the procedure. I'd seen the doc do this type of thing enough times to know that the pulse would disappear under the inflation of the cuff but was supposed to reappear when deflated, revealing the systolic blood pressure; I was not reassured as he repeated it yet again.

"Doc?"

He removed the cuff and tossed it to the side. "*Gott* . . . Her blood pressure is dangerously low." Pulling the plastic curtain aside, I watched helplessly as he reached in and felt the girl's neck, even going so far as to feel around on her throat. "Swelling at the jugular because the superior vena cava is being pinched off and unable to drain into the heart, causing tracheal deviation—crackling feeling of the skin at the neck from the air that's under there."

Steamboat shuddered and swayed to the left, and tremors sounded through the fuselage as I held the doc as still as I could. "The pneumo-thing-a-ma-jiggie?"

His eyes came back to mine, and I could read the trepidation in them. "Yes. The volume of a gas is inversely proportional to the pressure to which it is exposed. So, as barometric pressure falls in the aircraft cabin during the ascent, trapped air in the pneumothorax causes it to expand by approximately thirty-eight percent upon ascent from sea level to the maximum *cabin altitude* of eight thousand feet." He shook his head.

"It wasn't noticeable in the helicopter because their cruising altitude was much lower, whereas in our unpressurized cabin the pressure is whatever it happens to be." He laid a hand on the gurney. "Her problem is worsening."

I thought about the conversation the doc and I had had when we'd boarded the plane. "What about the syringe needle deal?"

"Evidently the wound is too great; we'll never be able to withdraw that much air on a continual basis."

I sighed. "You know what I'd like, Doc?"

"A Pleurovac?"

"Well, besides that. I just want one break—just one thing that goes right on this flight." I processed what he had just said and yanked my face around to look at him. "What kind of vac?"

"A Pleurovac."

I shook my head. "Please tell me we have one."

"We do not."

I couldn't help but make a growling noise. "How long does she have?"

"I don't know, but the airspace in her chest cavity is growing and has collapsed the lung; it's now crowding her heart, Walter, to the point that it will no longer be able to pump the blood needed to keep her alive."

I set my jaw. "Well, we're going to have to get all *western* on this, aren't we?"

"What does that mean?"

I glanced around, looking for something that might resemble a Pleurovac, undeterred by the fact that I had no idea what one looked like. "We've got to rig something up."

He stared at me with his mouth agape, horrified. "Rig something up? Walter . . ."

"She's going to die, Doc."

His voice was sharp as the bomber kicked to the side again. *"Ich berucksichtige den!"*

"English, Doc." My eyes rested on a small apparatus attached to the gurney, and I nodded toward it. "What's that?"

He shook his head, dismissing the thought. "Nasogastric pump; it's connected to the hose that is running through her nose and down her esophagus. It decompresses her stomach and keeps her from vomiting and aspirating while she is on the ventilator."

"Can we take her off that and use the pump?"

"And if she aspirates?"

"Doc, you said her heart isn't going to be able to take the pressure, so she's dead if we don't do something . . . Maybe she'll throw up or maybe she won't." I looked down at the small body. "She's got a strong stomach—I mean she's hung in there so far."

I watched as one of the most intelligent men I knew coaxed his intellect out onto the thin ice of speculation, a place where I worked and lived. "I can use the tubing from the nasogastric pump and I have medical tape . . . But I need a container, something with a lid—with liquid in it."

"What kind of liquid?"

"Doesn't matter."

I stood there for a second, feeling every mile an hour we were traveling—and then glanced toward the front of the plane. "I'll be right back."

"What?" The doc's voice called after me as I shimmied onto the roof of the bomb bay and crawled toward the cockpit.

In the rush to get there and because of another bout of turbulence, I bounced off the radio section and fell to the floor near my seat as both Lucian and Julie looked down at me, the Raider the first to speak. "Where in the Sam Brown have you been?"

I ignored him and reached a hand up to his copilot. "Julie, I need your water jug."

She pulled it out and handed it to me with a confused half-smile. "You thirsty or nervous?" She studied my face. "Or both."

12

I watched as the doc carefully removed the plastic tubing from Amaterasu's nose, produced a scalpel from his medical kit, and cut the length of clear plastic in half so that he had two tubes. He hitched one end of one tube to the small turquoise pump that he had previously turned off and handed me the other end as we knelt on the walkway. "Hold this and keep it clean."

"How do I do that?"

"Don't drop it." He pinched one end of the second piece of tubing and made three oval-shaped incisions a quarter-inch wide, starting about an inch from the end in one-inch intervals, and then also handed it to me. "This is the end that we'll insert into her chest."

I motioned with the other tube connected to the turquoise pump. "What about this?"

"Just don't drop it."

The plane bucked again, and I took the moment to rest a shoulder against the gurney. "Got that." I looked back at the girl's grandmother, her eyes wide as she watched us, and I adopted the most professional air I could with only two months of being sheriff under my gun belt. "Routine medical procedure, ma'am."

The doc looked at me. "Now I have to make the Pleuro-vac." He picked up the opaque plastic jug. "This is perfect, Walter."

"I'm glad to hear it, because it's the only thing we've got."

With his surgeon's precision, he used the scalpel to cut two tiny, circular holes in the jug's plastic cap and inserted the other end of the modified tubing that had been slit into the jug, a couple of inches into the liquid. He then took the free end of the tubing that he had inserted into the pump and pushed it inside the plastic container as well, but only allowing it to reach the air portion of the half-filled bottle. "There." I watched as he began stripping medical tape from a roll and sealing the tubes where they entered the jug.

Having done enough drug busts, I knew paraphernalia when I saw it. "It's a bong."

He stared at me. "I don't understand."

"Nothing. Now what?"

"We insert that end of this tubing into her chest."

I handed it to him. "Maybe you'd better do that."

"Yes." We both stood as steady as we could, and I threaded the tubing through my fingers and grabbed the back of Isaac's pants again. "I'm assuming we need to be steady on this, right?"

He nodded, peeled the plastic tenting back again, and then pulled on a pair of plastic gloves and pushed the hospital smock up, his fingers searching. "I'm looking for the midaxillary line extending from the middle of the armpit down the side to her hip, bisecting the fourth rib."

"Are you telling me this because there's something I'm supposed to do other than keep the end of the tubing clean?"

He shook his head. "No, I'm talking to settle my nerves."

"Then keep talking."

I watched as he rubbed on a local anesthesia. The butt end of the scalpel rose as the doc grunted. "I'm making the incision through the skin and the fat and using my index finger to push through the tissues and down to the rib."

I figured if the doc kept talking in detail, I was going to be the one to aspirate, but I remained silent, biting the skin at the inside of my mouth and glad of the respite we'd gotten as far as turbulence was concerned.

Isaac used a pair of giant tweezers to separate what I assumed were the muscles in the girl's rib cage. "So far, I've been able to avoid the blood vessels and nerves that run to each rib, but I'm having trouble getting through the intercostal muscles and the parietal pleura . . ."

I swallowed. "If you must . . . English, Doc."

"The tough membrane that lines the chest wall."

"Right."

"I'm stretching and tearing the pleura and intercostal muscles to make room for the chest tube . . ."

"The one I'm not dropping?"

He nodded, still intent on the work as another kick came and swayed the aircraft just a little. "I'm using my finger to make sure I'm in the right spot and clearing the hole of any obstructions."

I glanced at Mrs. Oda, who had her eyes closed, which I thought was good thinking on her part, with her hands clutched together in what I assumed was prayer. "Let me know when you need the tube, Doc."

"I need the tube." Glad to relinquish the last of my responsibilities, I released his pants and handed him the end, trying to ignore the blood on his gloves as he hunched back over the small girl's body. "I'm threading the tubing beside my finger and upward into the anterior chest wall, toward her neck about five inches or so . . . This lays the chest tube on top of the lung in the space with the tip up by the highest point of her lung so that the air might drain most effectively."

I took a breath, the first I'd been aware of taking for quite some time. "We're done?"

"No."

"Damn." I blew out the breath and steadied the doc again as the plane bucked and sashayed a bit more. "Now what?"

"I'm suturing the incision around the tube and wrapping the ends of the suture around it multiple times, tying the knot so that it's secure and won't pull out."

He finished the job and then straightened, laying the tools of his trade aside and taping the tubing to the girl's skin, just a little away from the incision.

"Now we're done?"

"Not quite." He reached down and flipped the switch on the small pump and reddish bubbles began moving through the chest tubing into the opaque water jug, bubbling up through the water and turning it pink.

"It's supposed to do that?"

"It is." Grabbling the blood pressure cuff, he wrapped it around the tiny, limp arm again, pumped it up, and slowly released it—and all I could think was please don't let him pump that thing up twice. Instead, he lowered her arm and just stood there. I was about to say something when he turned to me, tears in his eyes and a smile on his face.

"Oh, Doc."

"Mind you . . ." He peeled off the gloves, snatched off his glasses, and scrubbed his eyes with the thumb and the forefinger that had just been inside Amaterasu's chest cavity. "The tube end is far from sterile, even if you didn't drop it, but I'm sure they can deal with that at Children's Hospital when she is no longer actively dying." He glanced down at the gurgling bubbles as they flowed into the plastic jug. "Note: none of this MacGyvered contraption is sanctioned by the FDA, the AMA, or any entity with medical knowledge or a modicum of common sense."

"I thought you didn't watch TV."

He leaned on the gurney, apparently exhausted. "*MacGyver* and Alistair Cooke's *Masterpiece Theatre* are the only shows I watch regularly."

"Thank God."

After checking her temperature, pulse, and other vitals before turning to Mrs. Oda and then me, he clarified, "It's possible that the temperature is helping, but with the complexity of medical attention she needs, an hour will be stretching it."

Glancing at the grandmother's distraught face and smiling at her to try to provide some sort of comfort, I got Isaac back in his seat, and draped the harness over his shoulders and around his waist as more turbulence struck the plane. "You stay here and keep this on. I'm going to check on our ETA."

Mrs. Oda tried to look like she might've understood what I was saying, and Isaac nodded but looked like he might pass out at any moment. "Hey, you did good, Doc."

I pulled out my pocket watch with the Indian-chief fob only to find that the glass face was cracked. It had been a gift from my father from his father before him, and in all the years

I'd worn it, it had never broken. Refusing to take it as an omen, I stuffed it back in the pocket of my jeans and dissembled just a little for the sake of everyone's spirits. "I'm betting we'll be there in less than an hour—Lucian said we were making good time."

Steamboat lurched again as if trying to take part in the conversation, and the doc was quick to grab his seat with both hands. I fell back against the bulkhead but got hold of the railing when the thing righted itself. Straightening my hat, I remembered the headsets. Glancing around the compact space, I finally spotted a set hanging in one of the holes in the fuselage braces. I reached up and took it down, placing a cup against my ear and adjusting the mic to my mouth. "Hey, I want my frequent flyer miles back."

The gravelly voice grated over the wires. Static. "Tough."

"Isaac bumped his head, and we had a little medical emergency, but everything's okay back here now. I'm going to hand the headset over to him so he can keep in touch."

Static. "Good, then get your ass back up here."

I didn't like his tone. "Why, is there something else wrong?"

Static. "Fighting this storm, we're using the hydraulics—I need you to get back up here and pump the handle."

"Roger that." I handed the headset off to Isaac and gave him and the grandmother a jaunty thumbs-up. "Duty calls." I gestured for the doc to put the headphones on. "Keep those things on, that way we'll know what's going on back here."

He adjusted them over his head and pulled the mic down to his mouth. "How do I talk?"

I was about to tell him, with my accumulated knowledge, that it was voice-activated, but could see from the look on his face that the commander-in-chief up front had already conveyed that fact.

I turned and started up the ledge and over the bomb bay. About halfway across the top, I became aware that the surface felt colder than before and that the tiny crawlspace seemed even louder. Ignoring that and anxious to get back to the red lever, I pulled myself along just as *Steamboat* decided to do a little more hanging and shaking, until I finally fell into the back of the cockpit.

This time I rammed against the defunct radio panel, some loose equipment falling from the surface and battering the top of my hat, brand-new no more. There was another pitch to the side and then a sharp drop. I swallowed and listened to the two engines fighting gravity and the wind and could imagine very clearly the fifty-year-old bolts that held on the wings.

"Well, are you going to get your ass up here and man the pump or are you going to sit back there in coach till we auger in?!"

He was snapping a look at me when another gust must've hit us broadside, causing *Steamboat* to shimmy, drop a wingtip, and then groan back into a momentary stable position.

Scrambling forward on my hands and knees, I crawled into my jump seat, attached my harness and headset, and began pumping like an oil derrick. After a moment, I raised my head and could see both Julie and Lucian were now leaning in and staring at the gauge he had told me was the indicator for hydraulic pressure. All I could think as I continued pumping was *Please don't let him reach up and tap that gauge.*

In slow motion, his finger came up and poked the tiny, round glass surface like a suspect. "We're still losing pressure."

Julie's voice came over the headset as she shook her head. "Why now?"

The old Raider glanced back at me. "When he pumps, we gain it back, but I'm thinking the engine devices finally gave up, leaks are draining the system, and we've picked up too much drag somewhere. The air speed indicators have lessened twenty knots."

The plane dropped again as if hit by a blacksmith's hammer, and I watched as the two of them struggled to straighten out the B-25. As I continued to pump, I remembered the freezing surface of the crawlspace and the extra noise I thought I had heard on my return trip from the back of the plane. "Would having the bomb-bay doors open cause that kind of drag?"

They both turned to look at me.

13

I have, in my time, been the instigator of many a harebrained idea, but none as bad as the one that was now racing through my mind. "Rick was beating on the bomb-bay doors with a rubber mallet to get them closed; he said that the hydraulic pressure leached from the system and that the doors sometimes opened with the lack of pressure and then get stuck down." The plane rose, then dropped and shifted sideways this time, like we were sliding on a slippery road of wind—my least favorite form of turbulence gleaned from a long list. "While I was in the back we must've lost enough pressure for them to open and now they're stuck."

Lucian steadied the yoke and stared at the instruments. "There's not enough leading-edge on those doors to cause this kind of drag."

Julie's mouth stiffened. "There would be if ice was building up on them."

"Is there any way to crank them back up manually?"

They shook their collective heads.

"Is there any way to get into the bomb bay?"

Lucian spoke this time. "No."

Julie made a face and then laid a hand on his arm and interrupted. "There is, though; when they retrofitted the plane as a slurry bomber, they put a hatch in the back of the compartment down near the belly." She glanced back at me. "I'm sure of it. I opened it when we were trying to track down the leak in the hydraulic system."

"How big?"

"Big enough to crawl through." She studied me. "At least I could."

Lucian's voice carried annoyance. "Then what the hell are you going to do, Troop?"

I thought about it. "Rick said there was a bar in there, locked to the side . . ."

Lucian laughed. "The tow bar for the nose gear?"

"Yep, that's it."

"And what are you supposed to do with that?"

I started unbuckling my safety harness. "Beat the ice off the doors. You and Julie can take turns on the handle and keep the pressure up while I try and get them loose."

Julie shook her head. "Walt, that bar is close to six feet long and it's locked in the fuselage—you'd have to hang halfway into the bomb bay just to reach it."

I tapped Lucian's leather-covered shoulder and noticed the captain's insignia on the epaulettes for the first time. "Well, given the limitations of our fuel situation, can we make it to Stapleton with the excess drag?"

He looked at the gauges and then back to me. "No, but I don't see how havin' you fall out the doors at over two hundred miles an hour is going to benefit us."

I stood as another shake-rattle-and-roll hit, turbulence that felt as if we were ricocheting down the barrel of a gun that forced me to grab the backs of both of their seats to stay erect. "Look on the bright side; you might lose two hundred and thirty pounds of cargo." I hung my headset on my seat and started back, just as Julie caught my hand.

She pulled something from her coveralls underneath her jacket and handed me the elastic headlamp she'd been wearing in the hangar, along with her safety goggles. "You better take these; it's going to be like the inside of a cow down there and maybe the glasses will protect your eyes from the cold a little."

I nodded thanks and then stepped onto the shelf and pulled myself along on the rods into the belly of the beast.

Thinking about what I was doing, I listened to the wind and noise in the compartment below me and could feel portions of the anatomy between my legs rapidly seeking cover in my rib cage. Hopefully, the compartment would be shielded from the wind enough that I wouldn't turn into a gigantic sheriff-cicle before I could get the job done.

Everyone was as I'd left them in the rear compartment of the Mitchell, but Isaac spotted me crawling out of the darkness. "Are we there?"

"Not exactly." I stepped down and seated myself, glancing beneath the back ledge at the hatch on the bottom of the bulkhead. It looked just big enough for me to fit through, but the idea of opening the back of the plane to a gale-force blast of arctic air onto the girl didn't appeal to me. "Are there any more blankets?"

Isaac shook his head. "No."

Steamboat bucked again, and I placed a hand on one of the

perforated braces; waiting till the turbulence settled, I cast an eye past Mrs. Oda, still harnessed into her seat, her eyes very wide. I spotted some cloth bunched on the floor toward the back of their compartment. "What's that stuff?"

Isaac looked at the discarded fabric. "I think it's the quilting that used to be attached to the walls before they put up this exotically designed padding."

I studied the branded pattern on the seafoam vinyl. "Maybe Eisenhower wanted to be a cowboy." I stepped past him and inclined my head toward the child's grandmother. "It is pretty swanky though."

"I just wish the quilting was still there—we could use the insulation." He hugged his arms around himself. "What are you doing?"

I dragged a couple of pieces of the olive-drab material toward the front. "I'm going to need your help." I grinned at him. "For a change."

14

The doc couldn't believe what we were doing, and neither could I, really. As I studied the clasps on the hatch, I tried not to think about how much Isaac Bloomfield weighed: probably 150 pounds, moderately damp.

Pulling the covers up over my shoulders, I turned to him, seated on the floor with me. "Stuff these in the hole after me and then sit on my legs when I get halfway in there. I'd just as soon not fall all the way in, if you get my meaning."

"Won't you be sucked out the hatch?"

I stared at him. "Nope, that's just if the cabin is pressurized and this one isn't; besides, we're not going as fast as a jetliner, but I can still fall out and be a horrifying surprise to guests on the third floor of the Historic Virginian Hotel in lovely downtown Medicine Bow if you don't hang on to me."

He looked at the hatchway. "I don't think this is a very good idea, Walter . . ."

I set my hat on the floor of the bomber brim up—I was going to need all the luck it could hold—and stretched the elastic headlamp onto my head. "If you've got another, now would be the time to voice it—I'm not really thrilled about the prospect, either."

Preparing to sit on top of me, he grabbed the quilted material and took a deep breath.

I flipped up the collar of my sheepskin coat tight around my neck and pulled on my gloves and the safety glasses Julie had given me.

He nodded, his face tense, his eyes wide behind his glasses. "How will I know when to pull you in?"

I smiled as best I could under the circumstances. "Don't worry; you'll be lucky if I don't climb on top of you getting back in here." I took a deep breath and then reached up and turned the headlight on. "Ready?"

"As I'll ever be."

I turned and began undoing the hatch. "Let's try and show a little more enthusiasm, Doc."

"I'm just trying to think of what I'm going to tell Martha, Cady, and Henry Standing Bear if I drop you."

I sighed. "Positive thinking, Doc. Positive thinking."

The blast of air from the open hatch was like diving into an ice rink, and my breath stuck in my throat as I pushed the thing to the side. It was, as Julie had said, as dark as the inside of the proverbial Black Angus.

As we banked I cast the beam from the headlight around, finally spotting the inside edge of the fuselage underneath me, just before my eyes smeared over with tears, half freezing and blocking my view even with the goggles.

I reached down and, against every instinct of self-preservation, pulled myself into the bomb bay; I could easily see the otherworldly, low passing cloud cover, or scud, as the pilots would have said, obliterating my view through the open doors. The wind was piercing as I felt Isaac sit on my legs a little early. I could feel his excited grasp around my knees as I inched forward.

I turned my head to the left, the headlight illuminating the spot where I'd seen Rick place the tow bar, and reached down, but the slipstream snagged my hand with a glacial grip and slammed my forearm into the bulkhead. I snatched my hand back and tried to think quickly, knowing I had a limited time in which I could withstand the cold. My face was already numb and my vision was deteriorating even more as I pushed myself farther out of the hatch with Isaac pulling in the opposite direction.

That's when the turbulence really hit.

Steamboat, like any good rodeo horse, sensed that there was a rider in a tough predicament and decided that now would be the time to take advantage of the opportunity to kick up her heels.

The B-25 must've dropped a good hundred feet; at least that's what it felt like. My hips battered against the hatch opening, I bounced and fell forward, spread-eagled, my hand actually resting on the inside edge of the bomb-bay doors.

The plane shimmied to one side with a bone-crushing jar and then rose and slipped sideways as the winds hit us again like a southbound freight—I had became a connoisseur of turbulence.

The breath I sucked in iced my lungs, and now I couldn't feel my head at all.

Isaac was doing his best to hang on to me, but his grip,

tenuous from the start, was now around my lower legs, and I was pretty sure he had his feet pressed up against the bulkhead inside.

There was no way the diminutive doctor was going to be able to pull me back in, so I was stuck with plan A and turned my head as best I could, spotting the bright aluminum surface of the tow bar against the chromate insides of the bomber.

I spider-walked my gloved hand up, still keeping some pressure against the constant wind, careful to not let any part of my body fall into the blistering slipstream that would, most certainly, yank me from *Steamboat* like an ineffective human bomb.

There were more tremors as the Mitchell began a series of shuddering jolts that felt as if we were driving over a washboard road.

There's always a moment when you're in a situation like this, where you think that now is the time to turn mother's picture to the wall, and I was thinking that if all this shaking and jolting hadn't loosened the doors enough to allow them to close, what the hell good was I going to do?

But my hand was resting on the tow bar now, and as I slid it just a little forward, I could see the latch that held it. My thumb was like a broom handle when I leveraged it against the clasp, but amazingly enough, the thing flew up and the aluminum rod came loose.

The forked tip dropped just a little and the slipstream caught it, sending the other end up into my nose, almost knocking me out cold. My other hand instinctively came loose and grabbed at the thing just as another fit of turbulence hit and the plane veered sideways.

I felt myself slipping out into the void just as another set of hands grabbed on to my legs. It was just enough to give me the time to jam the tow bar into one of the doors to give me purchase, so I started to try to knock away some of the ice that had built up on the leading edges. It was like pounding on a concrete sidewalk, but parts of it started to fall away and I felt like I was making small progress. I continued chiseling like a jackhammer, pretty sure that the effort was the only thing that was keeping me from falling out.

I glanced to my right, the safety goggles fogging but the headlamp illuminating a small movement in the hydraulic strut that operated the doors. Figuring it was my last chance, I forced the tow bar up and beat it against the canister, only the adrenaline in my body still keeping me going, and watched as the angular curve of the doors swept up like a mother's embrace to shut out the freezing sky.

I hung there for a moment, trying to get some feeling back in my face and arms, finally lodging the brace in the framework of the doors. Reaching inside my coveralls, I grabbed my handcuffs, securing one side to the tow bar and the other to a crossbeam, making sure that the damn things didn't open again.

Careful to not put any of my weight on the doors, I threaded my way backward and finally fell into the cabin with the quilted material folded around me. I slumped against the fuselage and welcomed the relatively warmer air into my lungs.

After a moment, I pawed the material away and watched as Isaac reattached the hatch and turned to look at me, his glasses crooked with one ear paddle resting on the top of his head, once again revealing the swelled lump. "My God, Walter, I thought we'd lost you."

I smiled, sure my frozen face was giving the impression of rigor, and the words fell from my mouth in broken chunks like cubes from a tray. "Me. Too."

He leaned forward. "You're bleeding."

Looking at the dark stains on the leather of my gloves, I brought a hand up and then drew it back as he dragged the medical kit toward him and reached for my face. Trying to push him away, I attempted to sit up. "I'm okay."

He pushed me back. "Stop being an idiot. I think your nose is broken—it is only the cold that is keeping it from swelling."

The words mumbled from my thawing lips as another wave of turbulence attempted to overturn us, causing the plane to rattle like a low-pitch maraca. "Good, it might ruin my boyish good looks."

I watched as he rummaged through the kit, ripping apart some gauze and rolling it between his fingers, finally reaching over and knocking the headlamp and goggles from my head and expertly tilting my noggin back. He wiped the blood from my face and mustache and then inserted the gauze in my nostrils. "There, that should at least staunch the bleeding."

My head lolled to the right and there was Mrs. Oda, squatting on my other leg, grasping my jeans as if I might still fly out the hatch and disappear. She was so light I hadn't felt her still sitting there.

She smiled, and I could see tears tracing down her face again.

I sighed and studied her—eighty pounds, soaking wet.

I blinked, but the plane seemed to swoop and wallow, the insides of the aircraft seeming to melt away and then reassemble themselves. I tried to focus my eyes, but nothing seemed to work, so I blinked again, every time becoming more difficult to open them. My voice sounded nasally and muted as I struggled to form words. I could feel the world around me attempting to slip away, and I didn't have time for that. I shook my head, which did nothing to help it feel better, and then focused on the elderly woman's face.

"I know I told you to stay in your seat, but I'm really glad you didn't."

15

"Where the hell have you been?" He studied me closer. "And what's in your nose?"

"I had to hammer the doors with my face but got them held shut with the tow bar and my handcuffs." I handed the headlamp and the goggles back to Julie. "Thanks, they were handy."

I seated myself as she released the hydraulic handle, glanced at Lucian and then me, and massaged her bicep. "That thing is murder."

"Tell me about it."

Her eyes went back to the old Raider. "How are we doing?"

He nodded. "The drag's gone, and we seem to be maintaining pressure." He turned to look at me. "But the fuel situation is worse than we thought; we lost a lot with those damned doors open." As he spoke, the left engine started backfiring loudly, and he looked at Julie and grimaced. "Next time, don't ask." He shone the flashlight on the offending motor. "It's iced up—we're going to have to shut it down, but we're almost to the Colorado border and if I make a jog to the east I think we can descend without hitting the Brown Palace. Get on the radio and let Denver Center know we are declaring an emergency and are turning to a heading of zero niner zero descending to seven thousand five hundred feet."

Lucian shut down the left engine, and the resonance of the propellers turned to one but the noise got even louder as he pushed the good engine's throttle forward to make up for lost power. As the old sheriff turned *Steamboat*, I heard him mumble, "Let's hope that's the only one we lose."

Julie held up her map and started talking to a notepad on her lap. "According to our NAV radio this heading will put us south of Cheyenne. Denver Center says that puts us east into warmer temperatures, but Stapleton is reporting high winds at fifty gusting to sixty-five knots out of the west and drifting snow. The cloud bases are eight thousand with temperatures of, um . . . forty-seven degrees!" Looking up from her notes, "Forty-seven degrees, how could that be?"

"Must be Denver is really having that Chinook, Toots." He shook his head. "Those damn things can happen anywhere up and down the eastern face of the Rockies from northern New Mexico all the way up through Alberta. Their warm winds damn well melt ice in a hurry—lakes can lose an inch an hour." *Steamboat* side-stepped again, and I watched as Lucian looked around as if it were a personal affront. "Crazy bitch of a storm, but we already knew that."

I readjusted the packing in my nose, which did nothing to get rid of the headache that was starting to build behind my eyes. "We're going to make it, then?"

"Not really." Julie's voice had a note of finality. "We

might make Greeley or Fort Collins, but there's no way we'll make it to Denver, even with the warm winds."

"Can we get the girl into Denver from there?"

She shook her head. "The AWC says I-25 is closed, even to emergency vehicles."

"What about secondary roads?"

"Walt, as bad as it is up here, it's even worse down there." She glanced at Lucian. "Anyway, Stapleton doesn't matter— the favorable runway is closed with drifts, so unless they get it open soon, I don't know how we're going to land this thing with the kind of crosswinds they've got, forty knots at least, Chinook or no Chinook . . ."

The old Raider's voice broke in, sure, steady, and perhaps a little annoyed. "We'll make it."

I stared at the side of his face. "Greeley or Fort Collins?"

"Denver."

Julie looked at him, the disbelief on her face writ large. "Lucian, not meaning any disrespect, but it's physically impossible; we're going to be way gallons of fuel short. With that engine shut down and the right side at max continuous power, our fuel burn is out of sight."

"We'll make it." He turned back toward the windshield and peered through the dark smudges of black clouds when his attention was drawn to the bucking horse charm that hung from the canopy. I think it was the first time he'd noticed it, and I watched him take the thing between his fingers, to test the golden metal, perhaps beseeching the trinket for a little luck. He fingered the cone-shaped, fancy-dance bell, and I'm sure it was the pistons in the engine shutting down, but just in that instant I thought I could once again hear drums— ancient drums, persistent and primeval.

"Do either of you know the difference between anxiety and fear?"

He glanced at Julie and then back at me, and I felt like I was in a classroom. I shook my head, thinking the drumming was a leftover from the concussion. "Lucian, let's try and stay focused here, shall we?"

He studied the bucking horse and rider in his hand and ignored the shuddering thumps of the wind. "I am focused; I'm more focused than you are. Now I asked you a question—do you know the difference between anxiety and fear?"

He took his gnarled hands from the yoke of the B-25, giving Julie a chance to absorb the impact of the next windy salvo; I guess he thought she needed something to do besides being the plane's unofficial Cassandra.

I nodded. "Yep, I think I do—"

"Anxiety is something generated by a feeling that you might not succeed. Fear is something else—that is what you feel when you are in an inextricable position." He smiled that matinee-idol grin of his, and I wanted to punch him. "You know who said that?"

Julie's eyes watched mine, and she looked at Lucian and me, not sure which of us had been concussed. "No. I don't, Lucian, but—"

"Jimmy Doolittle said that to me on the deck of the USS *Hornet*, the night of September 17, 1942 . . ." His voice tapered off but then gathered itself like the turbulence that rocked *Steamboat*. "I was anxious. Hell, I don't know . . . Maybe I was scared." He turned as if we were having a casual chat in the front seat of a pickup truck. "It was late and we were all supposed to be in our bunks, but I was concerned about my ship, so I went up on deck and walked to the flight line where she was tied down—almost like those navy boys had to make sure all sixteen of those birds wouldn't fly away on their own." One of his hands came up and took his glasses away, as if they were blocking his view of the past. "It was wet; fog so thick you could'a cut sheep out of it with shears. I guess we were about three-quarters of the way between the Midway Islands and Japan." He sighed to himself. "People always ask what you think about in moments like that; what's going through your mind? Well, in those situations I've had only one thing go through my mind, ever: please don't let me be the one that screws up."

The buffeting continued, and Julie fidgeted, acting a little more nervous than before, now that she was in control of the aircraft. She stared at him and tapped a gauge—evidently it was catching. "Lucian, the fuel indicators are nearly empty."

The Raider ignored her and continued talking. "They told us that if any one of our planes hesitated in starting that the navy boys had orders to push them over the side; there would be no time for fiddling around and if the damn things coughed or sputtered, into the drink they went."

He felt in the pocket of his leather jacket, and I noticed the patch on the left chest, a particularly ferocious-looking lion crouching out of a white arrowhead in a red background, and above it, a well-worn leather name tag that read CON-NALLY. "Hell, I'd flown that plane in California, Texas, Missouri, and Florida . . . all over the country, and I damn sure didn't want it getting dumped into the Pacific." He shook his head. "Of course she ended up at the bottom of the East China Sea, but that was okay, that was after she'd done her job."

Julie pleaded. "Lucian, we have to find a place to land."

He thumbed some tobacco out of the beaded pouch the

Cheyenne Elders had given him into the old briarwood pipe. I knew the beaded design on that tobacco bag well—*Dead Man's Pattern* they called it—and I also knew the Elders spoke carefully when they said his given Cheyenne name, *Nedon Nes Stigo*—He Who Sheds His Leg. "See, when you're attached to a piece of equipment in that kind of mission it becomes a part of you and the only thing I could think at that point in time, while sittin' there on that tire of the left landing gear and looking up at those two Wright-2600-92, fourteen-cylinder, air-cooled, radial engines was—you better damn well start."

"Lucian—"

Ignoring her, he struck a match and lit his pipe even though the vague scent of high-octane aviation fuel pervaded the cockpit. "They did, and as the bow on that carrier lifted up on a wave, we took that bird off into the morning sky, turned, and headed straight into the Rising Sun."

Julie leaned forward to confirm her suspicions and then looked at him. "Lucian, the fuel gauge reads almost empty."

He shone his flashlight toward the left engine and stared at her as if he'd just remembered that she was there. "Restart number one."

She stared at him. "What?"

"In case you haven't noticed, she's deiced; eight thousand feet and descending, the warmer temperatures thawed this frozen turkey out. According to your ceiling report, we should drop below the clouds any minute, Toots." He reached up and—if I had not known the man, I would have thought the gesture was caused by nerves—tapped the navigation radio. "Which is a damn good thing since our VOR is so weak we lost reception at this altitude." He stared out the murky glass. Out there, somewhere, was Denver. "Reduce airspeed to a hundred and sixty." He turned to look at me as he leveled off the aircraft. "Miles per hour; I did that for your benefit."

Static. "Walter."

I stared at Lucian. "Yep?"

The old Raider looked toward the back. "That wasn't me."

Static. "Walter?"

I glanced up at the pilot and copilot, now both turned and looking at me. I cupped my own mic. "Doc?"

Static. "I need your help. Now, Walter. Right now, please."

16

Crawling through the bomb-bay space again, I became aware of a noise in the aft compartment that I hadn't heard before, which was, in itself, amazing since you really couldn't hear anything over the constant thrum of the engines. "What's that noise?"

Isaac was crouched by the gurney and equipment in front of an orange device with a complex array of dials and gauges and an oxygen tank. At the instrument panel a red light was beeping and blinking like the one on the desk phone I'd inherited from Lucian—the one I planned on getting rid of as soon as I got back to Durant.

"It's the ventilator." He struggled to get to his feet, and I watched as he steadied himself on the rail of the gurney and adjusted the dials, punching a button that reset the machine. He turned back to look at me. "Something is wrong, but I'm not sure what."

I stood up, and my nose throbbed more with the effort. "Do you still need me?" I nudged the doc. "Maybe that wasn't water in Julie's jug."

I got no answer, so I waved to Mrs. Oda, who was still strapped in her seat, and turned to look at Isaac as he checked the tube in the child's chest and then leaned back to observe the container on the floor, still bubbling the pinkish exhaust from the cavity in Amaterasu's chest. "So, Doc, what's the verdict?"

"Umm . . . Probably nothing."

Stretching my facial muscles carefully, I massaged my eyes and looked at the small face inside the plastic tenting. "Not on this flight."

As if on cue, the orange device began flashing its red light and beeping again.

The doc and I looked at each other. "It just keeps getting better and better, doesn't it?"

Isaac ignored me, reached down and reset the machine again, and checked the tube he'd inserted in the girl's chest as well, noting that it hadn't changed position in the last thirty seconds. His hands then adjusted the tube leading into her mouth. "This makes no sense; the ventilator has been working fine since we took off . . ."

"What does it do?"

"It breathes for her."

"We need that."

"Yes, we do."

"It's broken?"

I watched him thinking as he had during the last crisis. "It's possible, but not likely. There's also the possibility that there is another pneumothorax on the other side of her chest, but that's not likely, either."

The alarm on the machine came on again.

This time the doc let it beep but readjusted the dials on

the instrument panel, and I watched the red numbers leap to his touch. "There is a pump inside that sends out a predetermined volume of air through the tubing that runs through the endotracheal tube."

"The tube in her mouth?"

"Yes." He adjusted one of the controls. "We're on CMV, which in English stands for Continuous Mechanical Ventilation, that allows me to control her respiratory rate or how many breaths per minute she gets." He stared at the dial. "The average at her age would be eighteen to twenty-two, but it could be higher if she needs it, but why would that change now?"

I ventured an opinion. "We've had the tenting open; is it possible she's responding to the cold, stress, altitude?"

"No, it's something else." The doc shook his head. "Tidal volume . . ."

I leaned in and could see the girl's body moving under the blankets. "What?"

"Tidal volume is the amount of air entering her lungs by the breathful—usually about two hundred milliliters for her age and relative size." He checked the valve on the tank at the bottom of the machine to make sure that it was on. "FiO2, fraction of inspired oxygen hasn't been adjusted and she should be getting the proper amount . . . Peak End Expiratory Pressure is adjusted properly . . ."

"What's that?"

"It helps to keep the slightest amount of pressure that the patient has to breathe out against; it keeps the smallest airways in the lungs open even when she is exhaling."

I looked over Isaac's shoulder and could read the red number five on the digital display. "Then the machine is all right?"

"Yes."

"Then it's her." I watched as the girl's chest heaved, and even I with my limited knowledge of medicine could tell that Amaterasu was in distress.

Isaac reached across the girl's undulating chest and disconnected her from the machine. He reached into the hanging bag of miracles Velcroed to the gurney and produced what looked like a toilet plunger.

"What's that for?"

"It's a bag valve mask; if the machine can't tell me what is wrong and she is not getting air, then I will have to breathe for her manually."

He squeezed the bag in a rhythmical pattern, and I watched as he fought it for a while and then began using both hands. "What's wrong?"

"This isn't working either." He held the small body as her chest raised and lowered again as if her lungs were attempting to escape. "It must be the tube; it's obstructed."

"So, what do we do, replace it?"

Isaac pushed the unused equipment away but handed me the bathroom plunger. "We need a laryngoscope to place the tube under direct visualization."

"I bet we don't have one."

"We do not."

I watched as our patient, the reason we were here on this mercy flight, began the business of actively dying again. "What do we do?"

Without missing a beat, the doc's voice took on a drawl, not unlike my own. "We get *western*." I watched as he pulled the tape from around her mouth and began carefully pulling the tubing from her windpipe.

"This doesn't look so bad."

"Out is easy, in is hard." He removed the end of the tube and gestured for me to come closer. "You're going to have to breathe for her while I clear the obstruction in the tube."

"Okay."

"Place the mask over her mouth and squeeze the bag every five seconds."

As the doc kneeled down, I did as instructed, trying to ignore the heaving of Amaterasu's body and the tint of her skin. "Got it." I squeezed the bag, but she continued to convulse. "Doc?"

"Keep squeezing the bag."

"She's turning blue."

"Keep squeezing the bag! It's probably that her throat is swollen, but we have to try. And talk to her—keep talking to her."

"What do I say?"

His head whipped around, and he shouted in my face. "You'll think of something!"

Words, I needed words, but my mind was a blank, black and empty as the Plexiglas windows on the sides of the bomber. Slowly, I became aware of my right hand crawling inside my coat and dragging the small, leather-bound book from my pocket—if I didn't have words, I knew someone who had. The book fell beside her and popped itself open to one of my stalling spots.

I continued gripping the rubber balloon but lowered my face down to hers and read in a steady voice. " ' "Oh! captive, bound and double-ironed," cried the phantom, "not to know that ages of incessant labor by immortal creatures, for this earth must pass into eternity before the good of which it is susceptible is all developed. Not to know that any Christian spirit working kindly in its little sphere, whatever it may be, will find its mortal life too short for its vast means of usefulness." ' " I could feel the emotion choking my voice as I pumped the bag. " ' "Not to know that no space of regret can make amends for one life's opportunity misused . . ." ' " She continued thrashing, and the tide of sentiment stole my voice, causing me to croak out the next words as my arm covered the book. "Don't you do this to us; we've come too far and gone through too much for you to give up now." I brushed the tears away from my eye with a coat sleeve. "Keep breathing. I know it's hard, but you've got to do your part, little *Shining Over Heaven*." I flexed the bag again, but her condition didn't change. "Doc?"

"I'm working as fast as I can." He reappeared with the tube, pushing a metal stylet into the clear plastic and bending it in the shape of a hockey stick. Isaac crowded in, and I stretched my arms so that I could continue to seal the mask over the girl's face and pump the rubber bulb. He glanced back at me, and despite the temperature in the plane, I could see droplets of sweat forming on his forehead below the knit cap. "I'm not sure she's going to survive this, Walter."

I nodded and then felt my jaw lock with determination. "She's not going to survive without it, right?"

He mirrored my expression. "No." I turned, gently moving the mask away, and he began inserting his fingers down the girl's throat, the play-by-play automatically mumbling from his own mouth. "I'm feeling for her epiglottis with my index finger; it's a cartilage container flag that closes over the opening to the trachea when you swallow so that you don't aspirate . . ."

I could see Isaac was having trouble operating on the thrashing girl. "Is there another problem?"

He actually laughed. "Along with all the other difficulties

involved in this process, the swelling to her epiglottis has made the structure something akin to a water balloon and nothing feels as it should."

"Is there anything I can do?"

"Yes, hand me the endotracheal tube."

Fishing the thing from around the doc, I placed it in his other hand. "I didn't drop it."

"Good." He guided the tube between his fingers into Amaterasu's mouth and threaded it down her throat into her trachea. Satisfied that it was in place, he removed his fingers and reached down to reset the ventilator again.

I stood there watching those red digital numbers and praying to God that the damned thing wouldn't start flashing and beeping again. Laying a hand on the girl's shoulder, I watched as she quieted and then lay still.

It seemed like forever with the two of us standing there breathing the exhaust of the bomber creeping through the cracks, watching the instrument display as the numbers remained steady. Isaac sighed deeply, and his voice was tired. "She's breathing again."

There was another shudder, and I was glad *Steamboat* had held off shaking us like fleas as I placed a hand on his shoulder. "Way to go, Doc." He shook his head as he looked at the girl. "What?"

"I may have just robbed this young girl of the gift of speech." He cleared his throat, probably in empathy. "With the predisposition of having a swollen airway because of the inhalation burns, the swelling from the endotracheal tube, and her small size—there was a great deal of trouble forcing the tube through the space between trachea and the vocal cords." He looked up at me—"She may never speak again."

17

The lights on the ground became more sporadic through the cloud cover, and the condition in the air had done nothing but get worse. On orders, I was in the bubble in the front that had been reserved for the bombardier and spoke to both Lucian and Julie on the headphones that I found there. "I don't like this; I almost fell out of this thing once and I don't particularly like being in its glass nose."

Static. "Hell, its nose is in better shape than yours."

We had passed both the airport in Greeley and the one in Fort Collins while I had been physician's assistant, so here I was looking through the panes at the rapidly appearing and disappearing clouds somewhere between here and there. "I can't see anything; can I come back up now?"

Lucian's voice sounded like it had when he'd trained me back in the seventies. Static. "Keep looking."

"There's nothing . . ." As I spoke, a perfect picture of the ground below opened up, and I could see a few lights leading out in front of us. "I can see lights. Is that the airport?"

Static. "Nope, that'd be I-25, which is just what we're looking for. In conditions such as this I use IFR."

Julie's voice came over the headset. Static. "Instrument Flight Rules?"

The Raider laughed over the com. Static. "Hell no—I Follow Roads. We'll just trail along the interstate the best we can and then veer off to the left when we get closer to Denver."

I was transfixed by the view and just kneeled there looking out the glass at the frozen surface of I-25. The road was mostly covered with snow and there was no traffic, but just as I had that thought, I could see the illuminated blue tracers of a Colorado Highway Patrol car parked on an overpass, probably near the Estes Park off-ramp.

In that instant I saw the poor guy open the door and step out, probably looking for what it was that was making all the noise. I can pretty well imagine the effect of opening your car door and having a Mitchell B-25 fly over you at night, trailing a couple of metric tons of snow behind it like diffused vengeance.

He dove for the door of his car as we thundered over and then veered left, dumping what must have seemed like a couple of hundred pounds of snow in there with him as he desperately tried to get the door closed.

Static. "You can come back up now."

I crawled back through the hole in the floor and reseated myself as the old Raider removed the pipe from his mouth and casually banged it on the side of his seat, a noise I was used to hearing, even though I couldn't.

"Check in with Stapleton Approach Control, Toots; it's possible that they can hear us and get us oriented. And remind them we are LIFEGUARD with low fuel."

Julie's voice called out into the darkness above Colorado, and we all waited in hopes that someone, anyone, would answer.

Static. "LIFEGUARD Raider Lima Charlie—Stapleton Approach Control—confirm you have Stapleton Airport in sight."

I imagined the muscles on the side of Lucian's face bunching in his trademark, shit-eating grin. "Roger Stapleton Approach—LIFEGUARD Raider Lima Charlie—in sight."

Static. "Raider Lima Charlie—Stapleton Approach Control—cleared into Class B airspace, maintain six thousand eight hundred."

Steamboat's nose pointed toward the sky like Pegasus, and we climbed back up.

Julie peered at the gauge that was becoming my least favorite instrument, right after the one for hydraulic pressure; she raised her horn-rims and stared more closely at the gauge, finally dropping the glasses back on her nose. "Lucian, we are now, officially, out of fuel."

He reached up and tapped the instrument in front of her face. "By God, look at that, we are out of fuel; let's hope Rick gave us more than we thought and that those gauges read low." He glanced at her. "One-sixty, Toots."

She stared at him for a moment, and then I felt the nose of the Mitchell slowly dip as she leveled *Steamboat* and looked at him. "Now what? Click my heels and say there's no place like home?"

"Lower one-quarter flaps."

"What?" There was a backfire as one of the engines stumbled for a second. "Right engine's going—I told you, we're out of fuel!"

The old bachelor's eyes checked mine again. "I don't think the phrase *I told you* is ever very far from a woman's lips." He turned and made the adjustment himself, the wing flaps forcing the nose of the bomber down into a more level flight, different from the way we'd been flying in the somewhat nose-high attitude before. He leaned forward and looked past his copilot as the right engine sputtered again and then caught and settled out. "Fuel outlet is located in the forward portion of the tank." He sat back in his seat and winked at her. "Bingo, just gave you at least forty more gallons."

She shook her head and smiled. "Any other secrets about this Pterodactyl that you'd like to share with us?"

"There might be a few." He smiled back at her. "We'll see what pops up." There was some chatter in all our ears, and Lucian repositioned his headset. "At least the Denver VOR reception is getting stronger on our navigation receiver."

Static. "Raider Lima Charlie—Stapleton Approach Control—contact Denver Tower."

Lucian adjusted his mic. "Hey there, Stapleton. This is Raider Lima Charlie requesting Runway 26 Left or Right. We've got a low fuel situation and I'm not liking the crosswinds we've got on Runway 35."

There was silence in the headsets, and then ATC spoke again. Static. "Raider Lima Charlie—Stapleton Tower—Runways 26 Left and 26 Right are closed due to drifting snow, can you land at another airport?"

Lucian laughed. "Like what, the Denver Stockyards, or have you got that closed, too?"

Static. "Raider Lima Charlie, the length of Runway 26 Right is blocked by drifting snow. Runway 26 Left has a snowplow stuck with only two thousand feet cleared on the approach end, braking conditions nil. I'm going to have to reroute you . . ."

Lucian shook his head, assiduously. "Son, I told you I've got a medical emergency and a fuel situation here and rerouting is not an option; get that plow cleared 'cause we're comin' in hot, and by God we're comin'."

Static. "Raider Lima Charlie, are you declaring an emergency?"

"Damn right I'm declaring an emergency, and I'm telling you to clear that plow on 26 Left."

There was a momentary now-familiar sputtering in the engine to our right, the same noises it had made when it had begun running out of fuel before. Julie turned and looked at Lucian. "You have some more tricks up your sleeve?"

"Not for that."

I watched as he spun the yoke, taking *Steamboat* into a turn, Julie looking at him, incredulous. "Lucian, you can't steep-turn this aircraft with an engine about to quit!"

"Just keep our speed above one-forty-five and we'll bring her in on Runway 26 Left ahead of that plow: two thousand feet. Hang on."

She sounded exasperated as she cupped her mic to her mouth and warned the back. "Isaac, make sure you guys are hanging on back there."

The doc's voice on the com lacked enthusiasm. Static. *"Gott helfe uns."*

Lucian's head inclined, defying the airport not to be there as he glared out the windshield. "Follow my lead with that pretty left leg of yours, Angel, and we'll be A-okay."

It felt like we were wallowing in the air, and I was sure that at any moment we were likely to stall and fall to the earth like a ten-ton feather. As we got lower the field seemed to get hazier as the powder drifted across the lights.

The Tower controller broke in again. Static. "Raider Lima Charlie, you are not cleared to land Runway 26 Left!"

Lucian straightened out *Steamboat* and began his descent with what felt like my stomach leading the way. "Stapleton, I am on final approach to Runway 26 Left."

Static. "Raider Lima Charlie—Stapleton Tower—we have plows and emergency services vehicles on that runway. I repeat, you are not cleared for landing on Runway 26 Left!"

I watched as he reached down to the console between him and Julie and pulled a lever, locking it with a wire basket bracing. The engine on the right sputtered and then caught again as the nose lowered with the movement of the landing gear. Two out of three triangular lights appeared on the dash. "Well, you need to get out of my damn way 'cause I'm lowering my landing gear and heading in."

Static. "Raider Lima Charlie, you have snowplows two thousand feet down the runway!"

My ex-boss and mentor pulled off his earphones and tossed them behind him, bouncing them off my shoulder. " . . . Asshole." He glanced back at me. "Pump that handle; pressure has dropped and the nose gear is not down."

As I clutched the handle with both fists and resumed pumping like a metronome, the third light on the instrument panel started to flicker. Ahead, you could periodically see the flashing approach lights of Stapleton, but as Lucian had predicted, the gusting winds were playing havoc with *Steamboat*'s stability. They pressed against the fuselage, and when they lightened, the craft was flung to the right before the two pilots could correct it. Gusts thrashed us the other times, and it was looking more and more like we were trying to thread a needle with a sixty-eight-foot wingspan.

The Raider reached down and made more adjustments, and I knew we were committed. The engine to the left sputtered and kicked like its brother, and all I could pray was that the thing would hold out for another two minutes.

Lucian's voice broke over the intermittent noise. "Looks like we're going in on a wing, a prayer, and possibly a dead stick."

The motors labored and I know it was my imagination, but I kept hearing them sputter in agonizing death, the half-silence in the cockpit deafening as the arctic wind whistled around us like avionic ghosts fleeing a sinking ship. The only remaining sound as I looked up at the lucky charm hanging from the canopy was a distant and determined drumming.

18

"Keep pumping that handle; just because the runway is solid ice doesn't mean we don't need hydraulics to keep that nose gear down."

Pumping like a fiend, I took a chance and looked up through the windshield but couldn't see anything. We were in a sudden snow whiteout. There was a vague sense that the world outside the cockpit was lopsided, confirmed when Lucian adjusted the yoke and I felt the wingtips dip, rise, and then straighten. "I can't see anything."

His hands stayed steady on the controls, the VOR needle centered on the final approach course. "Me neither, but it's gotta be out there somewhere." He glanced at his copilot. "I don't want to come in too low, and we have to keep our speed up in these gusts; we're gonna be a little fast when we touch down. The wind is right off the nose so that's gonna help but the brakes will do no good on the ice. After we get down, when I holler NOW, I want you to stuff that left foot of yours forward and give us full left rudder; at the same time I'm gonna goose the right engine spinning us around to the left. When we get going backward give us full right rudder to stop the spin and I'll set full power on the left. When we come to a stop I'll shut ol' *Steamboat* down."

She nodded her head, the situation having robbed her of words.

I pulled my hat down tighter. "We're only going to get one chance at this, right?"

"One's all we need." He glanced at Julie again. "Toots, give me altimeter readings, would you?"

She studied the instruments as he continued to peer into the blowing snow that kept giving the impression that we were flying sideways. "Five hundred feet."

He smiled. "Well, let's hope we make it over the Purina Dog Chow plant."

"Two hundred feet."

Suddenly the blinking lights at the end of the runway leapt into partial view, along with the vertical white stripes stretching into a vanishing point ahead. "It's there."

"I see it." He eased the yoke back just a little until I felt a shudder go through *Steamboat* as he played out the flaps on the verge of stalling, and then eased the nose forward, just a touch. "Damn it, we're too steep."

Depth perception was difficult with the whiteout, and the situation wasn't made any easier by the blowing drifts that intruded onto the runway pavement along the edge lights.

Another gust chose that precise moment to broadside us, but Lucian had been prepared and expertly adjusted the flight pattern so that we were now passing over the blinking landing lights at the end of the strip. "I was training in Amarillo back in the days before weather avoidance radar and we got hit by a Gulf Coast storm. The antenna got fused by lightning, hail damage, heavy turbulence, snow and dust that made for this brown slush on the windshield, and I gotta tell you, I was ready to make brown slush in my Army Air Corps junior-aviator pants."

There was a mild thump, almost as if plumping a pillow.

"All my instructor said was, 'Buck up, things are going to get worse.'" He glanced back at me. "And they did."

I looked out the windshield and could still see nothing but a momentary flurry of drifting snow and the edge lights. "When are we going to touch down?"

He smiled and then blew out his breath. "We already did."

Julie turned and looked at him in wonderment, shaking her head, a gasping cry coming from her mouth.

It was at that precise moment that the front of a five-yard, dual-axle plow appeared about a thousand feet in front of us, the blinking emergency lights flashing, the vehicle stuck in a drift completely straddling the runway.

I watched in horror as it looked like all the work, all the chances we'd taken to get the little girl here were about to go up in a spiral of snow, wasted and useless.

As if on cue and without hesitation, Lucian hollered. "NOW!"

I'd forgotten the old Raider's instructions, but Julie hadn't and stamped her left foot down in full rudder as Lucian slammed the right throttle forward and the Wright-2600-92, fourteen-cylinder, air-cooled, radial engine roared like the lion on the old Raider's patch, causing *Steamboat* to spin left on all three of her wheels and seem to kick backward like a bucking horse at the snowplow that was all of a sudden behind us.

Lucian swapped throttles, strongly bringing in the left engine as the right one sputtered to a stop, out of gas. Julie rapidly kicked the rudder pedals in an attempt to keep up. *Steamboat* started a swerve back to the right, but Lucian drove the yoke forward and cut the throttles as the second engine coughed and died for the last time. This maneuver was not as gentle as the landing and the gyroscope-like spin caused *Steamboat* to canter to the left as we slid along, slipping on the portion of the runway that we had just come from.

His jaw was set. "I hope that's the only one of those sons-a-bitches out here."

As we slid off the side of the runway I grabbed the back of both their seats; the nose suddenly dropped, and it felt like the landing gear in the front must have collapsed underneath us, the nose scraping concrete. *Steamboat* lurched to one side and the terrible grinding noise subsided, but as we began sluicing along on a bed of snow at a good clip, the lights of something else wavered and shone in the powdered mess.

She slowed, struggling to get back up on her two good legs, but the momentum of the maneuver continued to push us forward toward the flashing lights ahead. Both Lucian and Julie were frozen at the controls, incapable of doing anything that might have an effect on our outcome. Like a train wreck in slow motion, a phalanx of snowplows bloomed out of the snow, five of them running in tandem, straight toward us.

Seeing the plane, they locked on their brakes, and I watched as they grew closer. The grinding noise returned as Lucian attempted to navigate the stricken B-25 onto the plowed portion of the runway, scouring away speed as the bomber slowly, ever so bone-grindingly slowly, slid to a stop. All of us rocked back and forth as *Steamboat* did a quarter turn and halted, her wingtip only inches from the blade of the fore-most truck.

I watched as the old Raider stared at the giant plows, their yellow lights intermittently racing across his face. "Jesus H. Christ, if that don't get your blood pumping, nothing will." He removed his glasses and then reached up again to fondle the lucky horse charm that he had hung back on the escape hatch, and then he glanced at Julie, who had yet to move. "I could use a drink, how 'bout you, Toots?"

19

The medical personnel from Children's Hospital assisted Isaac in transferring the girl from the crippled bomber into the waiting EMT van parked under the shelter of *Steamboat's* wing.

The surrounding vehicles provided a kind of additional windbreak as they lowered the gurney from the hatchway, careful not to upset the bubble that held the child.

I caught the doc's arm and asked, "How is she doing?"

He shook his head. "I don't know, but at least now we're going to find out."

"I'll meet you at the hospital."

He nodded, but said nothing more.

Lucian and Julie joined me as the med-techs opened the back of the van; Mrs. Oda hovered next to the gurney, breaking her vigilance for only a second. Her eyes scanned the three of us and then settled on Lucian before reaching out and grabbing his hands and kissing them. *"Arigato."*

Embarrassed, he broke away and gestured toward Julie and me. "Well, I had some help . . ."

Once again, she grabbed his hands between her own and kissed them. *"Arigato, arigato."*

He nodded, all the braggadocio, smart-aleck remarks, and flyboy witticisms lodged in his throat as she and Isaac followed Amaterasu into the van; the doors closed and they were swept away in a slipstream of powdery snow. "Well, I'll be damned."

We stood there for a moment, watching the van's emergency lights fade into the storm as a very large and officious-looking man in a set of insulated coveralls marched over in Sorels and looked at the underside of the bomber's wing. "All right, is she out of here?"

I turned and looked at him, the frigid wind blowing the collar of my coat against my grizzly, blood-smeared face. "Excuse me?"

He was wearing a trooper hat with the flaps folded down around his round face, which did little to disguise his considerable bulk. "The crispy-critter; did they get her out of this thing?"

I felt coolness in my face and steadiness in my hands. "Yep, she's gone."

He nodded and then yelled over his shoulder. "All right, let's get this piece of crap off my runway. Pull those blades over here and push this junk heap into the barrow ditch!"

I was just starting to move forward when something flew in from the side and slammed him against the still-functioning portion of the landing gear, causing him to bounce off the giant tire, slip on the slush at our feet, and then seat him on his ample ass.

With her cap pushed back on her head, her blond hair escaping from underneath, Julie Luehrman stood over him with fists at the ready. "You don't touch this plane with anything but the kindest intent."

The ground-crew chief looked at Lucian and me, but we were staying out of it.

Our copilot pointed toward the main terminal and at the lights above. "In ten minutes, I'm going to be sitting at the window of the 38th Parallel Bar, and I'll be sitting up there all night, watching what it is you do with our plane—and you better not put one more scratch on it. Do you read me?"

He looked at us again, but the return look I gave him let him know that his life was in his own hands. He paused for a second more and then hurriedly responded, "Yes, ma'am."

Julie stood there for a moment and then nodded and looked back at Lucian before throwing her flight bag over her shoulder and starting off. "C'mon, I'll buy you a drink." She turned and looked at him. "And stop calling me Toots."

Knowing an opportunity when he saw one, he scurried off after her but yelled back, "I told you, something happens to men and machines in these kind'a situations; I guess it happens with women, too." From the darkness, he added, "Hey, how are we going to get home?"

I raised a hand to the side of my mouth and yelled after him, "We'll find a way!"

From out of the darting snowflakes, the reply came. "We always do, Troop!"

I lowered a hand to the crew chief and helped him up.

Gaining back some of his dignity, he brushed a little of the snow from his coveralls and then glanced up at the terminal lights. "Think she means it?"

I pulled my cowboy hat down a little tighter onto my head and shrugged my sheepskin coat a little higher on my shoulders in preparation for the trudge across the runway, then leaned in over him so that he could get a good look at the blood dried in my mustache, my nose, and the wadding therein. "I wouldn't test her, if I were you."

I walked from under the wing toward the front of the aircraft and paused at the nose of the fuselage to reach up and pat the golden hooves of the silver plane. "Good girl, gooood girl . . ."

20

I'd gotten one more look at her through the windowed entrance of the ICU before a formidable nurse stepped between me and the swinging doors. "Are you Walt Longmire, one of the sheriffs that flew that poor little girl down here in this blizzard?"

"Yes, ma'am."

She gestured toward the nurses' station. "I think your wife is on line two."

"Uh-oh."

"She doesn't sound too happy."

I followed her back to the intersection of two hallways and stared at the receiver lying on the counter like a loaded gun. Picking it up, the nurse punched a button and then made herself scarce. "Hello?"

"You made it?"

"We did." I glanced up at the clock on the wall behind the counter. "It's two o'clock in the morning; what are you doing up?"

There was a pause. "Waiting for my husband to call me."

"I'm sorry, Martha." I sighed. "We got to the hospital a while ago, but I've been filling out forms and trying to find an interpreter and . . ."

"How is she?"

"I don't know; it's up to these guys now."

I could almost hear her nodding. "You did everything you could."

"Yep."

Another pause. "Henry stopped by late with his traditional ravioli and a bottle of really good wine." She chuckled. "We didn't drink it. And, he wanted to know if you want him to drive down to Denver when they open the roads and give all of you a ride home."

"That's all right; I'm sure the skies will be clear long before the roads are."

"Rick called from the airport and said that Julie copiloted you guys down there?"

"Yeah, she has two legs." I thought about the incident on the runway. "And I guess she's formed quite an attachment to *Steamboat*."

"Who?"

"The airplane."

"Oh."

I leaned against the counter, luxuriating in her voice. "How's the punk?"

"Asleep in bed, where all good punks should be." I listened as she adjusted the phone in the crook of her neck and wished I were there. She took a breath. "Henry says he can run me up to Billings for that doctor's appointment this Friday, so you don't have to worry about that."

I didn't say anything.

"It's nothing; I just want to get it checked out."

I still said nothing.

"Look, big guy, with the lifestyle you entertain I'll out-live you by a wide margin—count on it."

I could feel a heat building behind my eyes. "I do."

21

Children's Hospital in Denver was a lot bigger than Durant Memorial back in Wyoming, so the nurse was able to find me a sofa to sleep on in the lounge. I flew through my dreams that night, slipping and sliding on the wind like a giant, armor-clad bronc. There were no engine noises, though, just the cleansing sound of the wind slipping over my riveted, aluminum skin—along with the thundering of drums and horse hoofs.

I wasn't alone there in the cloudless sky; there was another ship flying along beside me, smaller and more maneuverable—wing-girl of my dreams.

Lucian showed up at about five-thirty, drunk as a monkey and escorted by two Delta pilots, one of whom was carrying the Raider's prosthetic leg, and a Denver city police officer who had volunteered for the perilous journey to the hospital after hearing what the old pilot had done. They apologized for his condition, but said everyone there had insisted on buying him drinks until he was legless.

After seating him on my sofa in the lounge and seeing

the star on my chest, the pilots handed me the leg and scurried out into a dawn that was struggling to rise in a full-blown Rocky Mountain blizzard.

The patrolman studied the leg and then me. "Are all Wyoming sheriffs certifiably insane?"

I answered in the affirmative, thanked him for delivering Lucian and all his parts, and then joined the old pilot on the sofa as the Denver patrolman chatted with the nurses.

"Where's Julie?"

His eyes refused to focus. "Who?"

"Toots."

He nodded and batted my words away with his hand. "Couldn't hunt with the big dogs, so she got a hotel room over at the airport—asked for one with a view of the runways; got one for us, too, but I figured you'd be here."

I nodded and brushed some of the melting snow from his hat and leather coat. "Is this your original flight jacket?"

He picked at a hole in the elastic inner cuff and then found his bobbling attention drawn to the lion patch. "Thirty-Seventh Bombardment Squadron." A finger came up and popped the felt surface of the vintage patch. "My ol' squadron." He said it again, reiterating the information. "My ol' squadron . . . A lot of 'em are dead now." He glanced around as if they might still be there, if he looked hard enough. "Swam to shore in it; copilot Frank died in the Jap prison camp in China . . . Hell, sixteen little ol' planes with one ton of bombs apiece—by the end of the war they were sendin' out five hundred planes a mission with ten tons of bombs apiece; then they finished it off with two planes and two bombs . . . Taught them Japs a lesson, though."

I stood there studying the drunk man for a moment and

then placed his leg beside him, took off his hat, and started to pull a blanket over him.

His hand came up and pushed mine away. "How's the girl?"

"I don't know."

He started to rise but stumbled a little when he realized he was missing a leg, his eyes darting around looking for the appendage that was under his arm. "Well, let's go find out . . ."

I rested my hand on his shoulder again in an attempt to keep him settled. "No, Lucian, let's not."

"Bullshit, let's go see . . ."

Ignoring his protests, I stripped the jacket off and pushed him back on the sofa, plumped a cushion under his head, and laid the battered leather A2 over him along with the blanket. "Plenty of time for that in the morning."

The lion patch was near his face now, and he pointed at it again in a slurring stupor. "Thirty-Seventh Bombardment, my old squadron." His eyes wobbled as they climbed to mine. "Figured we could use all the luck we could get." He expelled a burp/breath, and it smelled like a distillery.

I sat there for a while, listening to him breathe, aware that I was no longer tired, and also aware that it was Christmas Day. I pulled the antiquarian copy of *A Christmas Carol* out of the inside pocket of my coat that I had thrown on the chair and, cradling it in my hands, it opened itself again to where I'd left off and to sentiments I was evidently not meant to escape: ". . . no space of regret can make amends for one life's opportunity misused. . . ."

My father, the man who had given me this book, a gift from his father and his father before him, had once told me that it was not what you did in this life that you regretted, but the opportunities you allowed to pass you by. I liked thinking that we had all been very courageous but it was possible, as I'd explained to the medical technician back in Durant in the belly of *Steamboat*, that it wasn't that we had been so brave or bold, but that we'd simply traded one fear for another—afraid of what we were about to do for the fear of what we might not.

"How come you didn't tell me she was a Jap?" A scratchy voice and two dark eyes looking at me from under the brim of the Stetson I had pulled down over his face broke my holiday reverie.

I sat there in the lounge and thought about why it was I hadn't mentioned it. "I didn't think it mattered." His eyes juggled some more but stayed with mine. "Does it?"

He took a few more breaths before resting his face against the jacket, his eyes shifting to his name tag. "You're sure that's why you didn't tell me?"

"Yep."

The dark eyes slowly receded into the shadows. "Well, you should've."

I tipped my hat back and, figuring the bleeding had stopped, pulled the gauze from my nose. Thinking he was already asleep, I quietly said to myself, "And why is that?"

He startled me when the mumbled words traveled from under the bound brim of his hat. "Could've appreciated the irony."

EPILOGUE

She still clutched the garment bag close in her lap, and I could just see where the skin grafts had been done on her hands and where a few teardrops had fallen, marking the black vinyl. Her head rose, and she wiped the moisture from her eyes, gazing at the blinking Christmas lights outside the plate-glass window of Lucian's apartment at the Durant Home for Assisted Living, the whistling sound still accompanying her words, a vestige of her damaged throat from that car accident, decades ago. "I'm sorry."

I sat on the sofa next to Dog and watched Lucian scrub a hand across his face.

"No one told me the entire story until after my grandmother died—you see, my mother and father were killed in the accident and she never wanted to talk about it, so I didn't know." She hugged the bag even closer. "My uncle told me the story as best he could from what he'd pieced together in letters that they discovered in a cedar chest. She kept mentioning a sheriff, a man who had saved my life. I have the letters . . ." She loosened her grip and gestured with the bag. "And this."

Lucian lifted his tumbler and studied her.

"There aren't that many of these around, you know?"

The old Raider said nothing.

"It wasn't that hard; I mean there weren't that many men who . . ." She glanced at me and then back to him. "I knew there was a sheriff, but your age didn't match up with what I'd been told. I checked the rosters for the Doolittle Raider reunions and saw your picture and the name; saw that you were a small man . . . No offense."

Lucian sipped his bourbon.

"Anyway, I wanted to bring this back to you, and thank you."

His voice cracked like the ice in his glass. "For what?"

Her voice whistled in return. "Saving my life."

"Excuse me?"

She looked confused. "I want to thank you for saving my life."

In the silence, we listened to the muted Christmas carols in the hallway as the wind pushed against the plate-glass windows of Lucian's apartment just like that blizzard so many years ago. "Young lady, I don't know what you're talking about."

"For flying the plane . . ."

He shook his head.

"But . . ."

"That's a wonderful story, young lady, and I'm very happy that you were able to survive your ordeal—but if I had anything to do with that, it's not something I remember."

She glanced at me and then looked back at him. "You are Lucian Connally?"

He set his tumbler down and reached across the chessboard to snag the bottle. Pouring himself another liberal dose of medicinal Kentucky, he looked at me but spoke to her. "Yes, ma'am, and I appreciate the sentiment, but I just don't recall that event. You have to remember that I'm getting advanced in years and don't have the clearest recollection of things."

She took a deep breath and licked her lip in exasperation. "Are you telling me you didn't pilot a B-25 slurry bomber with a burned child from Durant to Denver on December 24, 1988?"

He remained immobile but then lifted his glass and took a strong pull. "I don't recall that, and it seems that would be something I'd remember."

She sat there for a long time and then suddenly stood. "I appear to have made some sort of mistake."

Lucian nodded, amiable. "Oh, that's okay; I do that sort of thing all the time."

She reached over and took hold of the winged back of her chair, looking almost as if she might faint. "I'm . . . I'm terribly sorry that I've wasted your time." I stood and stepped toward her, taking her hand and assisting in steadying her. "I, um . . . I should be going."

The old Raider rose from his chair and looked her in the eye, allowing a long moment to pass. "Well, I appreciate your coming by and I'm truly pleased that things worked out as well as they have for you."

She leaned on my arm, and I stood there with her holding on to me as I listened to the soft wind of her breath. "Yes."

"Safe trip home."

———

We stood in the hallway; Bing Crosby was crooning "White Christmas," but the young woman, Dog, and I were only partially listening to the song filtering down from the recessed speakers in the ceiling.

She stood against the wall with the garment bag still folded in her arms and the whistling in her voice aggravated by the emotion she was fighting to hide. "That didn't go as I expected."

"Things generally don't with Lucian."

Her eyes came up to mine, and the tears were freely flowing. "Why did he do that?"

I pulled a bandana from the depths of my coat and handed it to her, Dog following our conversation, understanding its importance as he moved past me and toward her. "Oh, it's kind of hard to explain, but he doesn't do well with thank you's, or anything with an emotional basis."

She reached down and stroked the big beast's broad head. "I just wanted to thank him."

"I know you did, and I'm sure he appreciates the effort."

She gestured with the garment bag again. "And give this back to him."

I sighed and nodded, looking at the scuffed toes of my boots.

Her hand paused on Dog's head as she looked up at me. "Were you there when he left me this?"

I shook my head. "No, when he woke me up the next morning he wasn't wearing it, but I didn't ask."

Her turn to nod. "My uncle says my grandmother was asleep in the room with me but found it lying at the foot of my hospital bed when she woke up."

I moved closer, leaning against the wall. "I guess he thought you needed the luck."

She smiled and wiped more tears away.

"Signature Lucian; he likes pulling off the miracle but not waiting around for the applause even years later." I slid closer, carefully placing a hand on her shoulder. "I think it might've been that Steamboat rubbed a little luck off on you himself."

"The plane?"

"Nope, the horse." I took a deep breath and spoke softly. "Do you know why he was called Steamboat?"

"No, I don't."

"He was a rodeo horse, a bucking bronco of legendary repute—anyway, he broke his nose early in his life and from that day forward he whistled when he breathed, like a steamboat."

She smiled and then covered it with a hand. "Like me."

"Like you." I smiled and watched as she continued to pet Dog, but then she stopped, composed herself, and sidled a few steps away as if she were leaving. "Don't you need a ride?"

She turned and shook her head. "No, it's just a short walk to the motel my husband and I are staying in; if it's okay, we'll pick up the car at your office in the morning and then drive the rest of the way to San Francisco in the next two days."

"Okay." I thought of Isaac Bloomfield sitting at a dying woman's bedside, still carrying the weight of thinking he had robbed a young girl of her voice. I took a step to catch up and nodded down the hall. "There's somebody else in a room over in the other wing of the building I'd like to introduce you to, if you have the time—someone I think would really appreciate talking with you."

"All right." She paused for a moment, then her slim hands unzipped the garment bag and pulled the vintage leather jacket from its protective cover to hold it out to me. It looked exactly as it had all those years ago—the captain insignia, the name patch, even the arrowhead with the lion looked familiar. "Could you give this to him?"

"I think he'd rather you have it."

She still held it out to me. "I'd rather not."

I dropped my head in submission. "Certainly."

She began handing it to me but then pulled it back. "But if you don't think he'd mind, there is one thing I'd like to keep, as a memento."

"Sure."

She unsnapped the front pocket of the old A2 and delved a hand inside, pulling something out and then handing me the jacket. "Please tell him thank you for me?"

"I will." I watched as she took a few more steps, holding her hand close to her body.

She stood there with her clenched fist at her side. "Just in case you or he are wondering, *Steamboat* is at Ellsworth Air Force Base in the museum, just outside Rapid City."

I thought about that night, and how the vintage aircraft had kept us alive with a little help from Lucian, Julie, Isaac, Mrs. Oda, and, I guess, me. "Maybe I'll throw him in my truck and take him over there to see her someday." I smiled down at Amaterasu. "Whether he likes it or not."

"I think maybe you should." Taking a breath, she paused and looked at the fist that had risen to her chest. She finally smiled. "I think the flight meant more to him than he'll admit." She stood there for a moment more and then extended her hand. Slowly she opened it for my inspection, and there lay the tarnished beaded and belled trinket that had hung in the canopy of the B-25.

Steamboat.